Other books by Greg Smrdel:

"Hurricane Izzy - An OBX Story"
"Trivia Night: Answers You Wished You Knew"
"The Andy Griffith Show Complete Trivia Guide"

You can contact Greg on his website at
 www.gregsmrdel.com

Published by Milepost 11 Publishing - 2018

Contents

Author's Note:

For years, people have been telling me to write my story. It's a story filled with triumph and sadness. But I guess everyone's is. I have tried several times to write this story, but never with any success, until now. The story was too personal. Too hurtful. I just have never been able to do it. This story is the story of my life. The story of my children's lives......partially. What you are about to read is not 100% real. I had to mix in some made up parts to go along with the true parts. It was the only way I could get the story out. This book is made of "Factual Fictions and Fictional Facts."

I would like to thank each of my children. They will recognize themselves in this book as Jamie, Eric and Savannah, though not their real names. I did try to capture their true personalities the best I could. Linda is real. Sue is real. Andy and Rachael are real. The real heroine in this story, grandma Pat, is for sure real. She is my mother. The Bennetts, the Grays and John Clark, you will recognize yourselves also. I hope I have portrayed you well.

As always, I want to thank my family and friends for the encouragement. Beginning with my wife Char, who is a constant supporter in all that I do. My writing and comedy friends: Gershe, Whelan and Jennifer Stephens Shenberger (you all may recognize your names in here).

There is no better place on Earth than the Outer Banks of North Carolina. I love this place. Peace. - Greg Smrdel

CHAPTER 1

The diagnosis was not good. As she sat there listening to the doctor, Linda Stephens expected the worst, and although she prepared herself the best she could; the words still hit her like a punch to the gut. She thought she was ready, but who could ever be ready to hear something like that? As she sat there stunned, in the cold, sterile room of the James Cancer Center at the Ohio State University, Linda was handed the exact same results, heard the exact same words, and braced herself for the exact same fight that her mother, maternal aunt and sister had all gone through before her. Each of those strong women fought hard. They fought bravely. They fought heroically. But in the end they all came up short, leaving behind husbands, children and siblings. The oldest of the women, her sister; just 36 when she died. Chris, Linda's husband, was at her side when the news was given. Just as Andy, John and Bob had been for the others. The emotions were mixed. Chris knew the past history was not one that would leave anyone optimistic, but if anyone was a fighter, it was Linda. There has been nothing in life that Linda had not beaten and she wasn't about to let cancer be the first. Chris would be by her side, day by day, hour by hour, minute by minute. He would be there for support, to be a cheerleader, to take care of their three kids, Jamie, Eric and Savannah. Jamie was the oldest at 10. Eric, the middle child was 8, and Savannah was the baby at 3. Their lives were about to change.

It was only nine short months ago that Linda's sister Sue had died of breast cancer. She left behind a husband; Andy and a 8 year old daughter Rachael. Sue was only 36. Now here is Linda, facing her own breast cancer fight at the age of 35. Her mother Polly died in 1967 at the age of 31. Linda who was only 5 at that time has only one memory of her mother. That single memory was of her mother being carried out of the house dead, after she lost her battle with breast cancer.

From the time that their Aunt Susie was diagnosed two years ago, Chris and Linda had their three kids in a program through the James Cancer Center called Kids Can Cope. The program taught kids who either lost a parent or someone close to them to cancer, sort out their feelings and how to generally cope with everything. Ironically, Chris and Linda, after having the kids in the program for two solid years now were going to end their participation, but now the three children were going to need it more than ever.

Linda fought hard. She battled for two, sometimes promising, sometimes heart wrenching, long years. Unfortunately, on November 22nd at 10:30pm, after being placed in hospice that very morning, cancer won. When it came to this family, cancer always won. Linda, wife of Chris, mother of Jamie, now 12, Eric who would turn 9 in 3 days, on Thanksgiving Day, and Savannah now 5, passed away at the age of 37. She lived the longest of any woman in her family.

The funeral had to wait a day because of the Thanksgiving holiday. The family not feeling very thankful that year woke on Friday, November 26th to a cold hard rain. Seemed appropriate for a funeral. As the procession left the church to the cemetery, it ironically passed the office building of the insurance company that denied her claim for a bone marrow transplant. It was "experimental" they said. It was not a clear cut cure for breast cancer they said.

Due to their denial, several fund raisers were put into place to pay for the surgery. As far as Chris and Linda's friends were concerned, no option was going to be denied. That included the "experimental" bone marrow transplant. In the end it didn't help, but perhaps it gave Linda a few more precious moments to spend with her husband and children.

Linda was laid to rest next to her sister Sue. It was a beautiful spot. Underneath a massive oak on a rise looking over the rest of the cemetery grounds. A cemetery that has been around since the 1800s. At least that's what some of the gravestones nearby indicated. Sue's husband Andy had bought the last four plots in the cemetery two years previous and had given Chris two. As Linda's casket was lowered into the ground, a large part of Chris was also buried that day.

CHAPTER 2

Thanksgiving having just passed and Christmas and New Year's were just now straight ahead, distraction this family desperately needed. Family and friends were abundant and they saw to it that Chris and the kids had everything they needed. Not just materially, but emotionally too. Chris being the type to hold things in, occasionally had the need to be off by himself, now more than ever before. He was now a single dad without a clue as to how to raise three small children on his own. This was never more evident than the day just a week after the funeral when Jamie's first period began. Chris found himself in the feminine hygiene aisle of the store completely lost. He had no idea what he was supposed to buy. Too many choices, all of them foreign to Chris. Grief is funny. It seems to choose strange times to appear. The feeling of grief hit Chris so hard at this point that he actually broke down and cried for the first time since Linda's death. Right there in the feminine hygiene aisle at the Kroger's. He felt so overwhelmed and alone, more so than he ever felt before. Luckily, a store clerk, a young girl, came by and she helped him choose the right product. The young family got through the holidays. Somehow. All the activities kept their minds off things. But Chris found out again that grief hit the hardest over the dumbest things. One day he opened the door to the hall closet and on the floor were a pair of Linda's shoes.

That very small thing was like a kick to the stomach. In the quiet of January, with all distractions behind him and nothing but winter in the windshield of life up ahead, that small, seemingly unimportant thing of seeing Linda's shoes had put Chris over the top.

He thought at that exact moment that he would never be happy again. Sure, life goes on and the kids will have their accomplishments along the way, but those accomplishments will always be tempered with bittersweet feelings. Feelings that their mother should have been there to see them. Chris will always be haunted by Linda's words to God just a couple months before dying. Begging Him, pleading with Him to not take her. She wanted to see her children grow. She wanted to see Jamie's first date, Eric's first car and Savannah's career choice. She wanted to see her children happy. She wanted to meet her grandchildren. All things that her mother, aunt and sister were not allowed to experience. And sadly, neither would Linda.

During all this Chris did not want his children to be looked on with pity. Nor did he want them to use their mother's death as an excuse for any bad behavior. He tried very hard keeping things as normal as he could. Yet in school they were all still looked upon as "the kids whose mother just died."

The next couple of months were about adjustments. Chris had to get the kids up in the morning and off to school. He had to make their lunches, help them with their homework and didn't have the ability to play "good cop, bad cop" when it came to discipline. He was on his own. He had to do all this while trying to maintain a job as well. Chris was the morning DJ at Capital 102, the rock station in town.

With his schedule, he would not be able to maintain a work and family life. There's no way he could be on the air at 6:00 am and get the kids off to school at the same time. Chris' Program Director, Doug Johnson, was a kind soul and allowed Chris to take a demotion to become the midday DJ while still maintaining his current salary. Luckily, the 10:00am-2:00pm air shift lent itself for Chris to be there for the kids, both before and after school.

As April came around, Chris grew into a deep funk. Was it a depression? He didn't know. He didn't allow himself the time to grieve or work on himself emotionally.

He didn't have time for that. He had to make sure his kids were ok. They maintained their counseling through the Kids Can Cope program, but Chris was on his own. With spring break around the corner, Chris thought that he and the kids would do well to get away for a week. Deep down he understood that "running away from his problems" was not an ultimate solution, but it was at least a temporary one, and for now he was doing everything on a day by day basis. Ultimate solutions would have to come later, but for now, the single father and his three kids were going back to his old stomping grounds; the Outer Banks of North Carolina.

CHAPTER 3.

The day after they got married in Avon Lake, Ohio, Chris and Linda
Stephens relocated to the Outer Banks. Chris had moved down six months
before their wedding and had established himself as the morning DJ on
Ocean 105. He rented a house and set up a home for both he and Linda.
Linda would move down and establish herself as the Personnel Director for a
rather large 17-store shopping complex that included the best restaurant in
the area. The shopping complex was visited by locals and tourists alike and
Linda was very good at her job.

The young couple ingratiated themselves with the locals and soon they
had a large ring of friends. At one point Chris's brother Mike had moved
down to the Outer Banks and moved in with the young couple. There were
good times. There were bad times. Normal for a young couple starting out.
But life was largely good. Two years into living on the coast, Linda had
become pregnant with the couple's first child. Jamie was born on August
29th in Elizabeth City at Albemarle Hospital.

Jamie was a true delight and a very good baby. She slept through the
night from the day Chris and Linda first brought her home from the hospital.
She made being parents very easy! Chris was so happy, although he secretly
wanted a boy, this little girl had very quickly become the apple of his eye.

Life on the Outer Banks was good. They were a young couple with a small child living in what had become Chris's own version of paradise. Chris had been vacationing on these beaches since he was a young child. The first time he visited he knew that he would one day live here. Of course, the Outer Banks was a much different place back then. The Bypass was a two lane road. There was just the one traffic light at Colington Road for the entire length of the beach, and the bridge at the Manteo-Nags Head Causeway was a drawbridge, not the tall bridge that allows boats to pass underneath as it is now. If Chris didn't time leaving his house in Nags Head in the morning just right, he would find himself late to work at the radio station on Roanoke Island in Wanchese because of that drawbridge. The fisherman would leave for their day's work early in the morning. They didn't care that the overnight DJ was never happy if the drawbridge made Chris late. Even when Chris brought him an egg and cheese biscuit from Hardee's as a peace offering.

Big changes came for the young couple. Linda had a miscarriage and then found herself pregnant again soon after, this time with Eric. Secondly, a radio station owner from Columbus came to the Outer Banks to vacation. He heard Chris on the radio and offered him a job as the morning DJ on his station. Chris and Linda didn't want to move back to Ohio, but with one child and another on the way, they felt like Chris needed to take the job that offered them a great deal more money. Almost three times as much as it turns out.

Chris, a very pregnant Linda and Jamie Stephens, packed their bags, said goodbye to their friends and co-workers on the Outer Banks and moved back to the Buckeye State. Their Outer Banks adventure lasted five years and they thought about moving back every day since.

The family settled into their new life in suburban Columbus. Chris took the reigns of the morning show at Capital 102 and Linda took it easy at home waiting for Eric's eventual arrival. They didn't have to wait long as Eric made his appearance into the world two months later on November 25th.

Life was uneventful for the young couple for the next six months. As it turned out Chris and Linda moved just down the street from Linda's sister Sue and her husband Andy and their young daughter Rachael. Rachael fell in line exactly between Jamie and Eric. A year younger than Jamie. A year older than Eric. All three kids becoming best of friends. A few years later, as a complete surprise to both Linda and Chris, along came Savannah to round out their family at five.

A few years after Chris and Linda moved back to Ohio the world changed for both families. Sue was diagnosed with breast cancer. She fought the disease for two long years before finally succumbing. Her last wish was to hold on long enough for Andy's 34th birthday. She did. She made it till the day after.

Nine months later Linda started her own unsuccessful fight.

CHAPTER 4.

Chris and the three kids arrived on the Outer Banks just as the sun was starting to rise on a Saturday morning. Chris liked driving through the night. That way the kids would sleep for most of the 10 hour trip. Thankfully, Chris's mother, the kids grandmother, had retired to Manteo, on Roanoke Island, giving them a free place to stay for the week. Grandma Pat, lived on the main floor of the large house she had built two years previous. There was also a large upstairs, with two bedrooms and a large sitting area and a deck on the back of the house overlooking the in ground salt-water pool. Since the April air was still cool, and the ocean too, the kids enjoyed having the pool that was heated to a very warm 90 degrees.

As they pulled into the driveway, Chris could smell the bacon and eggs wafting from the house as they were busily being made in anticipation of the family's arrival. Funny, Chris thought, when I was a kid, mom rarely made a big breakfast like that, but now that she had grandkids….

Grandma Pat came rushing through the door and down the steps when she heard the Jeep Grand Cherokee drive over the gravel in her driveway. She helped Chris wake the three kids and carry them into the house. The kids, surprised that they were already there, greeted their grandmother with a flurry of hugs and kisses, and with an equal flurry, they finished off the mounds of food waiting on the dining room table.

Chris gulped down several cups of coffee, it had been a long night for him. He then carried their bags up to the bedroom with Eric helping him. Grandma Pat announced to the kids that while dad slept for a few hours that she had the day planned out for them. After a quick clean up in the enclosed outdoor shower, they were off to the Roanoke Island Aquarium.

Grandma Pat was an interesting person. While Chris was away at THEE Ohio State University, grandma Pat was getting her degree at John Carroll University, a private Jesuit college in suburban Cleveland, Ohio. Chris used to always complain by saying "I can never use the excuse that college was hard, to explain my bad grades. I was in a Radio/TV program at the same time my mother was in Pre-law. I was struggling and she was killing it." All the while, grandma Pat had Chris' four younger siblings still at home to raise. Grandma Pat graduated John Carroll with honors and went to John Marshall Law School, graduating and passing the bar at the age of 50. She opened her own practice and helped champion women's causes, often doing pro bono work for the women's shelter in town. Now she was retired and doing volunteer work on the Outer Banks. One of those places she volunteered was at the Roanoke Island Aquarium.

The Aquarium was one of three in North Carolina operated by The Department of Natural and Cultural Resources, and had been since 1976. Grandma Pat and the three kids had an enjoyable few hours at the Aquarium, getting there just in time for the alligator program, where they brought out a live baby alligator for the kids to look at and touch. It turns out, much to nearly everyone's surprise, that alligators are highly intelligent and are trainable. Grandma Pat joked "See kids, there's still hope for your father!"

Jamie and Eric laughed, getting the joke, but Savannah did not understand why the others were laughing. She figured it, "just one of those older kid things." Grandma Pat then took the three on a behind the scenes tour of STAR, The Sea Turtle Assistance and Rehabilitation Center that the aquarium had set up.

The aquarium houses sea turtles that have been injured in some way, whether by a shark or a boat propeller and they nurse them back to health before releasing the turtles back into the wild. The three kids got to help feed the turtles their lunch. It was then that Eric announced to his sisters, grandmother and the staff of the aquarium that he wanted to be a marine biologist. It was at this point that Savannah had her an announcement of her own.. She announced that she had to go potty and that she was hungry.

Grandma Pat laughed and said, "Ok Savannah, let's get you to the restroom and then we'll go wake up your grumpy ol' father and grab some lunch."

When the group got back home to grandma Pat's house, Chris was already up and swimming with the pool tether in the back yard. The tether was a belt that you wore around your waist that was anchored to a pole mounted on the pool deck that allowed you to swim in place. As a kid, Chris was a swimmer, having swam for the city teams, the local YMCA and his high school. It was often the activity that Chris would go to, to decompress.

Once home Savannah yelled out while pulling on the tether rope, "Come on daddy, get dressed, we're going to lunch!"

Chris got out of the pool, dried off and got dressed, feeling much better after his nap and his swim. He threw on a pair of khaki cargo shorts and a Whalebone Surf Shop t-shirt and a pair of flip flops. The five went to Arnold's, the 50's style diner that sat on Highway 64 at the south end of town. Chris would have preferred the Lost Colony Brewery and Cafe, but he knew the kids loved Arnold's. Each table had its own jukebox. Not that the kids knew any of the songs on it, they just liked being able to select the music themselves.

The family got there right after the initial lunch rush had cleared out so a table was available right away. Grandma Pat's neighbor, Storm was their server. Storm and her single mother lived 3 houses down the street from grandma Pat. She just started at Manteo High School that year and Grandma Pat was tutoring her in a couple of classes and teaching her piano. Grandma Pat wouldn't take any money for doing so of course, so Storm would often times give her free fries or a Diet Coke when she came in for lunch. Storm figured the owner wouldn't care, since the owner was her mother Jennifer.

Grandma Pat introduced Storm to her three grandkids and to Chris, and they placed their order, while the kids were fighting as to who got to pick the next song to play on the jukebox. At the very next table over was John Clark, an old friend and an old boss of Chris' back in the old days of Ocean 105. Back then Ocean 105 was the Modern Rock station on the Island, today it's the Classic Rocker, once again playing songs Chris played for the first time years ago. It seems the station had come full circle. John and Chris remained friends through the years largely due to Facebook. Chris was genuinely surprised to see John sitting at the next table.

"Bro!" John called everyone bro. "Bro, you didn't tell me you were coming down."

"Yeah" Chris responded, "Just had to get away. Not much thought had been put into this trip. I was gonna call you tomorrow to see if we could hook up at some point."

"Absolutely, sure. I was going to call you this week anyway about something." "I'm really sorry to hear about Linda. You guys ok?"

John had been close with the couple when they lived on the Outer Banks. He was one of the people that Linda opened her house to on Thanksgiving. It was Chris and Linda's habit to host a big Thanksgiving meal for those at the radio station and the shopping complex that were home alone on the holiday. John being a life long bachelor was always happy to get the invite. It saved him from eating Chinese on Thanksgiving Day.

"Yeah. We're good John. Thanks". Chris said.

John knew right away that was a lie. Chris's eyes didn't have the usual sparkle. It seemed that along with Linda, something inside of Chris died too.

John finished up his lunch said his goodbyes to the kids and grandma Pat and reiterated to Chris to call him tomorrow, he did want to talk to him about something. Chris agreed he would and with that John was off and out the door.

Chris, Grandma Pat and the kids finished lunch and on their way out invited Storm and her mother Jennifer over for dinner. She was planning on making her famous low country boil. Both women readily accepted the invitation and the crew left and made their way to the Wanchese Seafood Industrial Park to get the necessary items for the dinner.

"What do you suppose John wants to talk to you about?" Grandma Pat asked Chris.

"I have no idea. It probably has to do with some girl." John was always asking Chris about some girl. It was as if the life long bachelor was always looking for some sort of excuse to get out of a relationship. She lived too far away, she was too needy, she was too independant, there was always something that John would conjure up in his mind. And often he would use Chris as a sounding board to practice his argument before the break up.

With items bought for tonight's dinner they all headed back for home. Grandma Pat suggested that Chris and the kids all go out back to the pool so they're not in the way while she gets things prepared for dinner. Chris and the kids got their bathing suits on and stayed out of the way. Chris grabbed the book he was reading, "Hurricane Izzy - An OBX Story," about a landscaper in Kitty Hawk and a hurricane that slams the Outer Banks. He and the kids then all headed down to the pool for a relaxing afternoon.

It was nice, Chris thought, to watch the kids play so carefree. Although it's only been five months since their mother died, it has seemed like a lifetime ago. The heaviness has laid on Chris' shoulders everyday since. Chris thought their get away would do them all good, but there was a very strange mixture of emotions boiling inside Chris right now. The Outer Banks, he often said, was the place that his soul lived. Physically he hadn't lived here in a number of years, but spiritually he's never left. Now, every street he turns down, every familiar face he encounters, every song he hears on the radio, brings up memories. Memories he had with Linda when they were a young couple just starting out in life. Of course now her life was over and Chris was left to raise their three children alone. The bitter sweet feelings of the Outer Banks were rushing over him like a tidal wave.

Chris was startled out of his thoughts when grandma Pat yelled out that she needed him to husk the corn for the boil. Jamie, excited to help said she would run and grab the corn and bring it down. Chris knew that she just wanted to use the elevator on the exterior side of the house to take her up to the main level. The house was built on stilts due to hurricane and nor'easter flooding and the kids loved riding up and down in it. Once the corn was husked Grandma Pat suggested that everyone get cleaned up and dressed. The neighbors would be over shortly.

The older kids got dressed and washed up while Chris helped Savannah pull some clean clothes out of her suitcase and got her dressed. While dressing, Savannah asked "daddy, are we going to see the house where you, mommy and Jamie lived? Jamie said she wanted to show me and Eric the house she lived in."

This was a road that Chris really didn't want to go down right now. He didn't want to go to the house, the memories he thought, would be too hurtful. But he knew that Savannah, ever the inquisitive one of the three, would hound him until he answered. "Yes princess, if you and your brother and sister want to go, we'll go." Deep down he was hoping the five year old would be too distracted while down here to bring up the subject again.

CHAPTER 5.

As Chris finished up in the outside shower, the neighbors, Storm and her mother Jennifer arrived at grandma Pat's house. Jennifer was a very attractive, sun kissed, surfer type girl, not much younger than Chris. Long blonde hair, long legged. Not that Chris noticed. The way he felt now, he would never notice a girl again. He had found the love of his life in Linda, and now she was gone.

Jennifer and Storm had moved to the Outer Banks from Richmond, Virginia approximately four years ago to open Arnold's. She had been raised in the restaurant business, her father owned several large, successful restaurants throughout Virginia. Jennifer worked in all of them in all capacities, from dishwasher to general manager. If there was one thing she knew, it was the restaurant business. What she didn't know, however, was the marriage business. She and Storm's dad were only married for a year before they split. He, at the time, was the third baseman for the Richmond Braves, a minor league baseball team, part of the Atlanta Braves farm system. He has since become a major leaguer having played for several teams, including the Cleveland Indians. Chris's favorite team and Chris was a fan. Small world, he thought.

After dinner Storm and Chris's three kids all went down to play and splash in grandma Pat's saltwater pool, leaving the three adults upstairs. The conversation, as it would be expected, was centered around their kids and their past marriages.

Jennifer never met Linda of course, but had heard many stories about her from grandma Pat. Jennifer said that she could tell that Linda was a first class wife and mother. Chris relayed a few stories about her ex that he had read about in the Cleveland newspaper sports section. Hell of a ball player; not much of a human being as it turned out. He's not paid any child support in nearly a decade now, despite making millions of dollars playing baseball. Jennifer never pursued it; she was just happy he was out of their lives. It was at this point, Chris was happy he didn't wear the number 28 Cleveland Indians jersey to dinner, the one sitting in his suitcase upstairs. He had no idea his favorite player's ex-wife lived down the street and seemed to be one of his mother's best friends, despite the age difference.

After finishing the second bottle of wine for the night Chris was wearing out fast. He did drive all through the previous night with only a quick nap that morning, so Jennifer grabbed Storm and they said their goodbyes to the three kids, Chris and grandma Pat.

"Well, if you're down for the week, I'm sure we'll run into each other again. If not, have a wonderful stay!" Jennifer said as she walked out the door for home.

Nothing like good ol' fashioned southern hospitality Chris thought as he closed the door. He missed that very much, having moved back to Ohio.

"Nice lady" grandma Pat said.

"Yes she is" Chris responded, not thinking much more about it. With that, he and the kids went upstairs. Chris tucked them in, told them a story about the wild ponies of Corolla and all four were asleep within minutes, their first day on the Outer Banks complete.

CHAPTER 6.

When you're at the furthest point east in the United States, the sun comes up a little earlier than it does anywhere else in the country. This morning was no exception as the sun came streaming through the windows. Chris woke to the smell of coffee brewing and bacon frying downstairs. Even though Chris was an early riser, a habit carried over from his days of doing morning radio, his mother somehow always managed to be awake before him.

"Morning ma" Chris said sleepily as he came down to the kitchen.

"Sleep alright?" She replied.

" I always sleep well here. Must be the salt air. Or maybe my body and my soul reunite when I'm here."

"We'll eat in about 20 minutes, go wake the kids up and get them ready." "Church starts in a little over an hour." Grandma Pat, just prior to Linda dying, promised her that she would make sure the kids would receive the proper religious upbringing. That was important to Linda, even more so the closer she got to the end.

Chris, although raised Catholic by his mother, who before meeting his dad, had thoughts of going into the convent, was not necessarily a religious man. He had gone to 12 years to Catholic school and that may have been the reason. Too many rules, too much "do as I say not as I do" mentality for his liking.

Though when Jamie was first born, he and Linda did have the argument that a lot of couples do that are of mixed marriage religions. She wanted to baptize their oldest Presbyterian; Chris wanted Catholic. Linda ultimately won the argument when she forced Chris's hand. She said "fine, Catholic it is. That means you have to take her to church every Sunday." So, Presbyterian it was then. Chris figured being Presbyterian was kinda like being Catholic Light anyway......

The kids up and breakfast devoured, out the door they went to the Outer Banks Presbyterian Church over on the beach in Kill Devil Hills (seemed an appropriate named city for the church). This was the church that Jamie was baptized in and where Chris and Linda's good friends JW and Bonnie belonged. They got to the church just in time and the kids were surprisingly not fidgety throughout the service. Afterwards, Chris, Grandma Pat and the three kids went to the coffee and cookie gathering at the end of service where they ran into JW and Bonnie.

"We were so sorry to hear about Linda" Bonnie said to Chris through her tears. "She was one of the greatest, most courageous women I have ever known," she continued. "She, nor you and the kids deserved this hand."

"Thanks" Chris responded. Although he had been told this numerous times throughout the months, he never really knew what to say back to people who expressed their condolences. For a guy who made his living talking, he was always at a lack of words in these situations.

Bonnie, when Chris and Linda lived on the Outer Banks, was Linda's best friend. They worked together at the shopping complex and the two couples socialized together. JW and Bonnie had two children of their own fairly close to age to Jamie, Eric and Savannah. JW was a successful contractor and had done some work on the condo that Chris and Linda lived in.

Despite the years and the miles that separated them, the two couples had maintained their friendship. In fact now, Bonnie who runs the kids at risk program for the county was friends with grandma Pat who did a good amount of volunteer work for them.

"If you're free tonight, we'd love to have ya'll out for a cookout" JW said.

"Ma? Are there any plans?" Chris asked.

"Yeah, there is" she said. "We're going to JW and Bonnie's! Thanks for the lovely offer. I'm sure that all the kids will enjoy getting together again."

With that both groups were off, agreeing on being over at JW and Bonnie's in Colington Harbour at 5:00 that evening.

In a hushed tone, Chris bent down to his mother's ear, "it just seems really weird to be getting together with them without Linda here."

Grandma Pat, ever the practical one responded with "I know Christopher," she was the only one who ever called him Christopher, "but this is your life now, and you're just going to have to get used to it. You don't have to like it, but you do have to damn get used to it."

On the way back to Roanoke Island, Savannah kept saying that she wanted to go back to the place "that has the music boxes on the table" for lunch. So on the way home, the group stopped once again at Arnold's. Jennifer was there playing hostess to the after church lunch crowd and led the group to a table overlooking the sound. Storm was off today, but another young high school girl took care of the family. Jennifer came over during lunch and sat with them for a bit. Grandma Pat told her they were going over to JW and Bonnie's for dinner. That's the beauty of living in this little beach community, everybody knows everybody.

"Oh, I love them" Jennifer said. "JW, did most of the work here in the diner for me when I bought the place." Originally, Arnold's was a car dealership with the same name. Arnold's Cars. Jennifer liked the name, it was reminiscent of the TV show Happy Days and decided to keep it. JW came in and converted the space into a restaurant for her.

"I'm sure JW and Bonnie wouldn't mind if you came with us tonight. I can call them" grandma Pat said.

"That's awfully sweet of you" Jennifer replied. "But with Storm off today I have to work a double."

"That's too bad." "But tell you what" grandma Pat said, "Call Storm this afternoon and let her know that we'll pick her up and take her, that way she doesn't have to worry about dinner tonight."

Storm also knew JW and Bonnie well. She was their two kids' babysitter.

"Deal!" Jennifer replied.

After lunch, the group made their way back home to grandma Pat's. Once there, the kids changed into their swim suits and headed down to the pool. Grandma Pat, a bit worried about her son's state of mind said to him "I got the kids this afternoon. Why don't you hook up with John or do something for yourself. God knows you haven't been able to do that for a while."

Chris smiled, thanked her and and agreed that some time alone might be a good thing. Having to always be strong for the kids, hadn't allowed him anytime to do any grieving yet. As he walked out the door, he heard Savannah say "grandma Pat, why hasn't daddy cried yet?"

Chris headed back across the Manteo-Nags Head Causeway to the section of beach that he and Linda would always go to near MilePost 11. Chris parked the car and walked out onto the beach, he traced the steps that he and Linda took almost nightly down to the Nags Head Pier. If Savannah saw him now, she would't have asked her question. For Chris had just become overcome with grief. He didn't think at that moment he was going to pull this single father of three kids charade off much longer. He felt like he was just getting by at best, and hoped that it didn't adversely affect the kids. The fact that he had no idea what he was doing.

Chris sat on the beach a good long while. He watched each wave come in and then go back out. Come in.....Go out. Come in.....Go out. He had this warm, remarkable feeling that Linda was sitting at his side. It was as if she was each wave coming in to meet him, but then going back out again. It was like she was saying, "although I'm not here in person, I will always be here in spirit, like the waves never officially leaving the beach, nor will I leave you." "Just come to this place of solitude in your soul, that's where you will find me." Chris had another good cry, then started his way back to grandma Pat's house.

Dinner at JW's and Bonnie's went well. Storm, Chris's three and JW and Bonnie's kids all got along very well and they had fun on the outdoor trampoline. Savannah was especially cute trying to duplicate the older kids moves, and Eric was very happy that JW Jr was there. He was tired of only having his sisters to hang around with. The evening didn't turn out as awkward as Chris feared it might. Perhaps being able to let go while on the beach that afternoon helped. Dinner was great, BBQ chicken, hamburgers and hot dogs. Everyone ate well, and as the sun started to set, the group said their goodbyes and Chris, grandma Pat, et al, headed back to Roanoke Island.

CHAPTER 7.

The next morning Chris got up before the rest of the house and put on the coffee. He was able to get half-way through his second cup before Savannah sleepily came out to the front porch. "Daddy, can we see your's and mommy's and Jamie's house today?"

Chris pulled his youngest daughter up onto his lap "Of course we can princess" he said.

"Daddy?"

"Yes, dear."

"Does mommy know we're here?"

"Yes, Savannah. She knows. It's hard to explain and even harder to understand, but your mommy knows everything now and watches over all of us." "She'll always be here with us."

"You mean mommy is here now?"

"Yes Savannah. She's here now…"

"Is she a ghost or something?'

"No, baby girl, this is the hard to understand part, she's not a ghost, but she's with you as long as you always remember her, she's in your heart." "You always carry her with you."

"You're right daddy, I don't get it. If I'm carrying mommy, why doesn't she feel heavy?"

Chris wanted to laugh and cry at the same time. The innocence of his youngest child, caught him off guard a bit.

"Daddy, I miss mom."

"Me too pumpkin. We all do. But you have a super power that me and your brother and sister don't have."

"Really?!?! What daddy?"

"You look just like your mommy, so whenever you miss her a real lot, all you have to do is to look in the mirror and you can remember her. That's a real nice super power to have."

Savannah, feeling proud at this moment that she looks like her mother and no one else did, caught her dad off guard once again. "Daddy, whenever you, Jamie and Eric miss mommy, you can just look at me, ok?"

"Thank you Savannah, that will be nice."

Just then, grandma Pat came out to the front porch with more coffee and some sweet potato biscuits. "Hey grandma Pat," Savannah said. "I got a super power that nobody else has."

"I'm sure you do sweetie". What is it?"

"I look just like my mommy and whenever I miss her I can just look in the mirror to see her."

"That's a very nice super power to have. You're one lucky girl!" "Here Savannah, have a biscuit and some milk."

"Yeah, I better grandma. I need to be strong 'cause I have to carry mommy."

Grandma Pat looked over at Chris with a quizzical look on her face, "Don't ask," he said.

Soon thereafter, the other two kids got up for the day and came down to the front porch to have their breakfast too.

Once done with breakfast, grandma Pat announced that she wanted to go take a walk on the beach and then do some grocery shopping. She asked if the three kids would come with her to help pick out meals for the last few days of their spring vacation. She figured that would give Chris the chance to follow up with John who still wanted to talk to Chris about something.

Chris really didn't want to be bothered with John's latest girl problem, but they have been friends for 25 years now and if John wanted to talk to him about something, then the least he could do is give him a few minutes of time. Grandma loaded the kids into her car and off they went across the Manteo - Nags Head Causeway towards the beach.

Chris looked at the clock. It was 9:30am. John goes on the air at 10. Chris thought instead of calling, he'd just go down to the radio station and sit in the studio with John while he was on the air. Besides, he hasn't been down to the old job in quite a number of years. It would be nice to see the place again.

Having a bit of time to kill before leaving for the radio station, Chris decided to get into his swim suit and get a few minutes of swim time in. He went out back startled to see Jennifer in the pool attached to the swim tether.

"Oh sorry, didn't know you were here" Chris said.

"No worries" replied Jennifer, "Your mother is so nice to allow me to come down here every morning before work to get 30 minutes of swimming in." "Here, I'll get out so you can have the tether."

"No, no, no, you stay and finish. I can come down here later and do this."

"Thanks" Jennifer replied. "I feel so much better when I get my swim in each morning."

"No worries" Chris said. "Have a great swim."

"Thanks, and Chris, make sure you bring the kids and your mother to Arnold's at least one more time before you leave back for Ohio. On me."

Chris agreed that he would and he took the elevator back upstairs to the main level of the house.. If he had to admit it, he liked taking the elevator on the outside of the house as much as the kids did. It's not something you do everyday. He made himself another cup of coffee and read the "Coastland Times" newspaper. Something about having an actual newspaper in your hands that Chris liked, rather than just reading the news online. Once finished Chris got dressed, and got into the car, turned on Ocean 105 and started out for his old stomping grounds.

John was already on the air when Chris pulled out of grandma Pat's driveway. The same music, now old, that was new when John and Chris last worked together almost 25 years ago, was the soundtrack for the ride. Brenda Russell's "Piano in the Dark" was playing as Chris pulled off Grandma Pat's street and out onto Highway 64. In the 15 minute drive from Manteo to the radio studio in Nags Head Chris listened to some of the music that brought back memories from his days of working at the station. People and bands like Joe Jackson, Steely Dan, New Bohemians and Chris's favorite; Bruce Springsteen. Chris smiled as he recalled the fights that he and John would get into as to who was better, the Boss, or John's favorite, The Beatles.

Chris pulled into the radio station parking lot. The studio was once on the south end of Roanoke Island in Wanchese when Chris worked there. A ramshackled old building built in the 1940s. Complete with a mobile home for the administrative offices. They are now in a beautiful new facility on the beach. Not a trailer to be seen anywhere on the property. Not even a double wide.

Chris walked through the 2 huge plate glass doors painted with the Ocean 105 logo. Ocean 105, it says, 'where life's a beach." The receptionist was a woman that looked very familiar, maybe just 25 years older now. Annie recognized Chris immediately and passed on her condolences about Linda. "We heard right after it happened. It was so sad."

Linda had been as much a part of the Ocean 105 team as Chris had been himself. As he thanked Annie for her kind thoughts his eye was drawn to the black and white picture hanging on the wall right outside the on-air studio. Annie saw that he noticed it and said "now Chris, you know we can't get rid of that. That picture has been hanging here for as long as any of us had worked here."

Chris got up to the picture, studied it very closely. It was like looking back into a time machine. Staring back was Chris himself, from 25 years ago. It was him and Greg, the news director at the time, standing on the roof of a concession stand as they broadcast the Manteo High School - Lake Mattamuskeet football game. Lake Mattamuskeet High School didn't have a press box large enough to hold the Ocean 105 play-by-play team, so they broadcast the game from atop the concession stand. What few people noticed in the picture, however, was that Chris and Greg were being pelted by rocks from the Mattamuskeet students.

Chris looked back to Annie and asked, "whatever became of Greg? We lost touch when I moved back to Ohio."

"That old buzzard?" Annie snapped back. "He got married. Married to the best looking gal on the beach, he did."

"That's great!" Chris exclaimed. "Who?"

Annie looked a bit peeved. "Me, ya bastard!"

They both laughed hard at that. Apparently the noise loud enough for John to have noticed from the broadcast booth. John came barreling through the studio door into the lobby, "bro!" "I thought you were going to call. I didn't know you'd make a special trip down."

"Well, it's been awhile" Chris replied. "Figured it was time to see how you celebrities live each day."

"Yeah, real glamorous, ain't it?" "Been no groupies hanging around since you left ol' buddy." "You in a hurry?"

"Not especially" Chris responded. "My mother has the kids. I get the feeling that she's been trying to take them off my hands while we're down here because she's worried about me being a single dad now."

"Such a shame. Such as shame" John said nodding his head. "Everybody on this beach loved Linda. It was you that we just barely tolerated."

"Yeah, I get that a lot" Chris said.

"Tell you what, let me pre-record my last hour of the show and then you and I can go grab some fish taco's over at Mama Kwans . On me."

One hour later, Chris found himself at the corner table with a Red Stripe in his hand and fish taco's ordered. "So you wanted me to call you" Chris said, "what's her name and what's the problem."

"Bro, you thought I wanted to talk to you about a girl? Well, I guess, now that I think about it, that is why I most often call you."

"It's not about a girl? I'm shocked. Then what's up John?"

"Well bro, first, let me say how sad I was to hear about Linda. She was one of the good ones."

" I appreciate that John, but that's not why you're taking me to lunch. It's been so long since you have, I'm looking forward to seeing the cobwebs in your wallet when they bring out the check."

"Nice one bro. No, I brought you to lunch to offer you a job. I know I can't pay you what you're making now, being the big city DJ that you are, but we're going to have the afternoon drive position open from 2:00pm to 6:00 pm and I'd love to bring you back to the Outer Banks.

"Uncle Danny's spot?" Chris blurted out. Uncle Danny Daniels has been the afternoon guy on Ocean 105 seemingly since radio was invented. Uncle Danny had been there years already when Chris worked at the station a quarter century ago. "Is he ok?" Chris further asked.

"Yeah, Uncle Danny is fine, he just wants to retire now that he's in his 70s." "After panicking about what to do, it was suggested that we bring back the only guy that ever approached Uncle Danny's popularity to take over his show. That's why we asked Lee Curtis, but when he turned us down, we asked 3 or 4 more people…..I'm kidding bro! You're our first and only choice!"

Chris taken aback by all this didn't know what to stay. All sorts of thoughts and feelings clouded his brain. He loved the Outer Banks, that much was a given. He had always looked for a reason to return, but what about the kids? How would they feel about being uprooted. Leaving their friends and schools? How would I feel about leaving Linda? As it stood now, Chris would go to the cemetery after getting the kids situated at school each day and have his breakfast with Linda at her grave site. Can I just leave her in a cemetery and move on with my life like that, he wondered.

All of this was what was going on in Chris's head. What he verbalized however was "John, I'm flattered. I'd have to think about this, long and hard." "I'm not sure what I'd do about the kids after school though. If I'm on the air from 2 until 6, they would be alone for several hours after school."

"I knew you would bring that up bro." "In fact, that's already covered. I had a conversation about this with your mom. I wanted to try and gauge what she would think your reaction might be to my offer. She already has volunteered to pick up the kids after school and keep them till you get off the air. She would help with their homework and make dinner for you all, and after eating, you and the kids would head home."

"My mother knows about this?"

"Bro, yes she knew! How do you think I just happened to be sitting at Arnold's when you came in for lunch?" "She and Jennifer orchestrated the whole thing to have it so you sat at a table next to mine."

"Well I'll be damned. I did not see that coming. And how did mumsy say I would react to your offer?'

"She didn't know. She knows how much you are drawn to this place. She knows that you always say you'd like to raise the kids here, but she also knows that you wouldn't leave Linda either."

"John, this is a lot to take in" Chris said. "When do you need an answer?"

"No rush on that bro. Uncle Danny is still here for a couple of months yet. His last day on air is scheduled to be the Friday before Memorial Day. Provided we've found his replacement by then. But I do need to fill the position at some point before that."

"I get that John. I really need to spend some time with this. Can you give me a couple of weeks?"

"Sure. No problem bro" as John got up to go to the bathroom just before the check arrived. He probably orchestrated that too, Chris laughed to himself.

Check paid, Chris and John were in the parking lot and ready to head their separate ways when Chris asked, "What about Uncle Danny? I'm sure he holds a certain responsibility to his time slot after he leaves. You don't do something that long and don't feel an ownership towards it. What are his feelings on a replacement?"

"He has only one choice for his slot, and it's you bro." "He's completely on board with you taking over and in fact, hopes that you can be there for a long, long time." "We haven't made his retirement plans public, so please don't spread that around just yet."

That weight that felt lifted off his shoulders when he arrived on the Outer Banks a few days ago, was now firmly placed back on. If Chris was a bachelor this decision would be easy, but he's not. He's a widower with three small children. Life isn't just about him anymore.

Chris got into his car and headed for Roanoke Island. He had Uncle Danny playing on the radio. The guy is a legend, Chris thought. How do you replace a legend? What if I flop and they fire me, then what? I'd be unemployed with three small children to take care of and no job. But then again, that scenario could also play out in Ohio too. So that argument doesn't hold water. The further he drove, the heavier the weight became. As he crossed over the Manteo - Nags Head Causeway, Chris watched as the seagulls swooped down to the water. He watched the fishing boats return to their moorings at Pirate's Cove Marina at the end of what was likely another successful fishing day.

As Chris eased the car into the driveway at grandma Pat's, out from the pool came rushing, soaking wet, his youngest, Savannah.

"Daddy, we had the best day with grandma Pat! We took a long walk on the beach. She showed us how to dig up sand crabs and we saw dolphins!"

"That's great sweetie" Chris said, answering his youngest. "Where's grandma now?"

"She's upstairs making us spaghetti and meatballs for dinner."

Chris made his way upstairs, using the steps this time rather than the elevator. "Have a nice talk with John, dear?" Grandma Pat said smiling. "Straighten out his girl problems for him?"

"Real nice, the woman who taught me never to lie, lied to me." Chris sarcastically replied.

"I didn't exactly lie" grandma Pat responded, "I just didn't correct you when you told me that you thought John wanted to talk to you about a girl."

"Touche" Chris replied.

"What do you think you want to do Christopher?"

"I have no earthly idea. If it was just me, I'd do it in a heartbeat. But I have 3 other souls I need to think about." "Do I have the right, or want to take them out of their schools, move them away from their friends, and not least important, deny them the ability to go visit their mother anytime they may want to."

"How many times have they asked you to go visit their mother in the cemetery?" "Or is it just you that only goes."

"They haven't asked yet, but that doesn't mean they won't in the future."

"Chris, I've been meaning to talk to you about that. You do realize that's not Linda in the grave, right? That's just her physical remains, her spirit and her soul are going to be wherever you and the kids are, whether that's here or in Ohio. Jamie told me that you go to the grave and have breakfast nearly everyday. I don't think that's healthy for you. At some point you have to move on."

Chris took it all in without saying a word. What his mother was saying was right of course. His brother-in law Andy had been telling him the same thing. It's only been 2 1/2 years since his wife died and he seems to be handling it much better.

"I don't know what to do. I need to think on this a while."

"I suspect you will" grandma Pat replied, "but I really think you should talk to Jamie, Eric and Savannah about this. I think their feelings may surprise you."

"You haven't said anything to them, have you?" Chris asked.

"Oh, no. I wouldn't dream of overstepping my bounds by that much. But having spent a good deal of time with them these last few days, I have a feeling they want and need to move past the sadness in their lives. I think they want to be just kids again, and not just be identified as the kids who lost their mother." "I also think its their father who isn't ready to push past the sadness yet. Almost like if he does, he's forgetting his late wife."

"There may be some truth to that" Chris admitted.

"There's nothing wrong with feeling sad" grandma Pat continued, "just don't let it consume you and affect every part of both yours and your three kids lives." "Linda was a wonderful woman, I loved her as my own daughter. And I do know this, because she and I had a conversation that you don't know about two days before she died. She told me to make sure you continued to live your life. I promised her I would not allow you wallow in self-pity over her passing, and that's a promise I intend to keep."

It was at that point that Eric came up the elevator and crashed through the sun room door and into the kitchen announcing that he was hungry and inquired as to when dinner might be ready. Chris always said about Eric that he'd rather "clothe him than feed him" since he was ALWAYS hungry and could seemingly wear the same clothes everyday, assured him that dinner was just minutes away. Chris told Eric to go back down to the pool and tell his sisters to come up, get dried off and changed.

CHAPTER 8.

All five; Chris, grandma Pat, Jamie, Eric and Savannah all sat down and made short work of the spaghetti and meatballs. Something about the salt air that always gave Chris a healthy appetite.

"Daddy, did you see your friend Mr. John today?" Jamie asked.

"Yes, dear I did". Chris responded.

"Did he have a girl problem?" Eric wanted to know.

"No boy." Chris had always called Eric, boy, and would often refer to him as "the boy." "Mr. John just wanted to talk about his radio station."

"You going to make his radio station better for him daddy?" Savannah asked.

"Better. Worse. I'm not sure". Chris replied.

"Well I know how you can make it better daddy" Savannah continued, "you can tell him to take all that old music off and put on Radio Disney instead."

"You're right pumpkin, that might be better than what he's got planned." "Enough about that" Chris continued "who wants to go climb Jockey's Ridge after dinner to watch the sunset over the sound?"

Jockey's Ridge is the most visited North Carolina State park covering 426 acres in Nags Head. It contains the largest active sand dune in the Eastern United States and is a favorite for all the people that visit the Outer Banks.

Jamie added, "I want to go, that way I can show Eric and Savannah where I lived when I was little."

From atop Jockey's Ridge you can see the Atlantic Ocean to the east and Roanoke Sound to the west. As you look to the sound and just a bit north, you can see a condo development called the Villas, which are perched right on the waters of the sound. That was where Chris, Linda, and at the time, baby Jamie all lived.

They all finished up dinner, helped grandma Pat with the dishes and piled into the car to head for Nags Head and Jockey's Ridge. Grandma Pat stayed behind because in her words "that's an activity you tourists partake in. Us locals, we don't go and climb that sand hill."

Chris knew better. Grandma Pat was staying back to encourage Chris to have a conversation with the kids about his conversation with John.

On the drive over, Chris still had Ocean 105 on the radio. "Wang Chung" by Wang Chung was playing,

"Everybody have fun tonight.
Everybody Wang Chung tonight."

That prompted Savannah to say; "see daddy I told you. This music is stupid. You should tell your friend about Radio Disney. All my friends listen to it."

Though he wasn't about to debate radio demographics with a 5 year old, and how radio advertisers aren't especially looking for 5 year olds with discretionary income to sell their goods to, he thought she might have a point.

They arrived at Jockey's Ridge in about 15 minutes. They unpiled from the car and started their trek up the large sand dune to the very top. The two older kids both ran ahead calling back "we'll see you at the top!" Savannah, sticking with her dad, to make sure he knew the way, she said.

At the top of Jockey's Ridge, the young family had the place to themselves. It wasn't quite tourist season yet, so there were few visitors on the Outer Banks at the moment. They all sat down and looked to the west. They saw the Villa Condo's where Chris and Linda once lived. Chris's stomach dropped to his feet as he recalled the days when he and Linda, and once she was born, Jamie, would walk to the top of Jockey's Ridge from their home to watch the fireworks on the Fourth of July as they were shot out over the Atlantic. From the top Chris could also make out the pier where he and Linda would throw a ball to their yellow lab and watch while she would dive in after it, swim all the way to shore, and then run the length of the pier, drop the ball and wait to do it all over again. Those were the carefree days. Days before breast cancer and death.

As they sat there watching the sun fall further and further down into the sound, Chris casually said "sometimes I really miss living here."

Though she really was too young to remember it, Jamie replied, "sigh, me too,"

Eric was the one to bring it up. He chimed in with "hey pops, do you think we can ever move here again?"

"Would you want to?" Chris asked.

In unison Jamie and Eric shouted "YES!"

Savannah, being the lone dissenter, said quietly, "if we move here daddy, I might forget mommy. I don't want to forget mommy."

This is exactly what Chris didn't want to happen. He vowed he would never let their kids ever forget their mother and now Savannah was proclaiming the same fear. But happily it was Jamie and Eric that had come up with the right answer. They both, in their own way of doing it, took their time to explain to Savannah that was never going to happen. Jamie, doing it the big sister way by saying "hey, sis, it doesn't matter where we are. On the Outer Banks, in Ohio or in South America, me and daddy will never let you forget mommy. She will always be with us."

Eric had is own way of reassuring his sister by saying "yeah, don't be stupid. You're not going to forget her. We won't let you." "Plus if you did, pops would probably ground you!"

Savannah, taking the word of her brother more to heart, than those of of her big sister, looked up to her dad with big soulful, sad eyes and said "would you daddy. Would you really ground me if I forget mommy?"

"Of course not sweetheart. But it doesn't matter because what your brother and sister say is right, we won't let you forget mommy. We'll always have lots of pictures of her around and don't forget that special secret power you have, that no one else has…."

"Shhhhh, daddy" whispered Savannah, "don't tell anyone about my secret powers."

Approaching the subject as carefully as he could, Chris brought it up once again. "Would you ever want to move here?"

This time all three agreed with a very hearty and enthusiastic "YES!"

"Does that mean we're moving here papadopoulos?" Eric asked.

"Well, I'm not sure" Chris answered. "Remember how I said my friend Mr. John wanted to talk to me about making Ocean 105 better? Well, he thinks he can make it better if I came back to work for him."

"Daddy you should go to work there" Savannah said with such excitement. "You can even use my idea about making it Radio Disney. I won't even care if you say it's your idea!"

"That's very nice of you sweetheart, but I don't think they want me to come in and change the station. I'm pretty sure they just want me to be one of the people on the air."

Now it was Jamie's turn to ask a question. "What time will you be on? Right now we can't listen to you because we're in school. You gonna be on when we're in school again dad?"

"Well right now I'm not sure it's even a good idea that we even do this. There is still a lot to consider. You have your school and your friends and your cousin Rachael back home too." "But if we do it, then yes you would be able to listen to some of the show. I would be on just before you get out of school until 6 o'clock."

Sounding worried Savannah asked, "who will take care of us after school?"

Eric put in his brotherly two cents again "you're being stupid again Savannah. Jamie and I will take care of things till pops gets home from work."

"Um, no you won't boy. *IF* we do this, then grandma Pat would be picking you up from school and taking you to her house. She would be helping you with your homework and making you dinner. I would come over after work, have dinner with everyone and then we would go home."

"We wouldn't live with grandma Pat? Savannah asked.

"Kids, I'm not sure we're even going to do this, but if we did, we might stay with her a short time until we found our own house." "No decisions have been made and honestly I'm thinking it's more likely that we won't be moving down here."

As the sun drifted further and further downward into the sound, Chris announced that it was time to go. "We need to get down the dune and back to the car before it gets too dark."

On the way back Eric, being as blunt as he usually is says "so pops, we're not moving down here. Why?"

"I don't know boy. I simply don't know."

The car ride back to grandma Pat's was a quiet one. Each one thinking their own private thoughts. Initially when Jamie agreed to moving down, she hadn't thought of her cousin Rachael. Rachael's mom Sue, was Linda's sister who had died two years prior to Linda. Jamie and Rachael had become unusually close for cousins, bonding by the fact they were both young girls without a mom to guide them through their teenage years. They had made a formal pact in the basement of Rachael's house the day after Linda died that they would be there for each other no matter what. Now her thoughts were concerning whether or not she was going back on that vow.

Eric's thoughts had also turned to doubt. This coming summer he would have aged up in his age bracket on his swim team. He spent all of last summer getting his butt kicked by the older kids, this year he was going to be the older kid and Eric was the one who was planning on kicking butt. If they moved down here, he didn't even know if there was a swim team. If there was one, he certainly didn't know where he would fit in. He already knew the answer to that question back home.

Ironically, the one who had been the lone dissenter in wanting to move to the Outer Banks was the one deep in thought as to how nice it would really be. Savannah rode in the backseat thinking how cool it would be that her daddy would be working at Radio Disney and how all the other radio people were going to think he was so smart because he came up with the idea.

Chris's thoughts? They were quite a bit more muddled. On one hand he would have the support of his mother, John, JW and Bonnie, something he did not exactly have back in Ohio. But it was also something too that may not be the best answer for the kids. This is when he missed Linda the most. She was the perfect sounding board and always came up with the right solution to every problem.

They eventually got back to grandma Pat's where they found her in the living room reading the book that Chris left lying out, the one about the hurricane, a landscaper and his girlfriend that lived on Roanoke Island. "Interesting book ma?" Chris asked as they came in the house.

"It's alright" she answered. "The author isn't any Ernest Hemingway, but nonetheless a good story about places I know down here."

"Hey grandma Pat!" Savannah yelled out as she came running into the living room almost knocking over a vase of flowers, "guess what?"

"What princess?"

"We might be moving here and daddy is going to make the radio station better by using my idea!"

"You're moving here Savannah?" "Daddy told you that?"

"Not all the way grandma. He asked us if we wanted to move here and that Mr John gave him a job, but we still might not." "But me and Jamie and Eric all want to!" "And he said you would pick us up from school and we could help you make dinner and you can do our homework for us!"

"Whoa. Whoa little girl!" Chris replied. "You got that a little mixed up, What I said was that Grandma Pat would HELP you with your homework, not do your homework."

"Oh yeah grandma. That's what daddy said. I just got a little mixed up 'cause I'm so excited." "But can you help me with something else too?"

"Sure sweetheart, anything."

"Eric said that daddy will ground me if I forget mommy. I don't want to be grounded, can you help me not forget her?"

"I would be honored to help you remember your mommy. I can tell you stories about her whenever you like."

"But what if we don't move here, how can you help me then?"

"Savannah, if you don't live here you just call me anytime you feel sad or lonely or if you want to hear a story about your mommy. I will always help you remember her no matter what."

"You're the best grandma, grandma Pat."

"And you're the best Savannah, princess."

"All Eric had to say was two words: "aw, puke."

It was a fitful night sleep for Chris. He knew that in the initial excitement the kids would want to move here, but when it all came down to reality, would they truly be ready and happy to do that? Jamie had a wide circle of friends at school. She has plans to join the on-air staff at her school radio station when she got to high school. She also wants to write for the school newspaper. Eric has baseball and swimming. He is progressing in both sports. He's a great fielding third baseman on the little league team and a pretty good butterflyer and IM'r on the YMCA and summer swim teams. Savannah was just coming out from the shadow of not having a mother. Is moving here causing another big stress on her life that she's not prepared to handle. These were all the thoughts that were hammering in Chris's head. He tried to look for some quiet, some solitude, so he could talk to Linda. He thought if he could say a prayer to her like he would to God that maybe she would provide the clear answer like she has always done in the past. Many a time Chris caught himself reaching for the phone to call Linda about a question that he had or to share something about his day, only to come to the stark realization that she was no longer there to call. So as Chris lay in the darkness and solitude of his bed with 1,001 thoughts firing at the same time, he turned over, face in the pillow and cried.

CHAPTER 9.

Rain came to the Outer Banks today. The kids had been hounding Chris about visiting a few of the souvenir shops to get a t-shirt of some sort to mark the occasion of their visit. Seemed like as good a day as any to do that since they'll be leaving soon to go back to Ohio.

"I'm going to see if I can find a shirt that says Outer Banks Princess,'cause that's what I am, right Daddy?" Savannah asked.

"That's dumb!" Eric added. "You should find one that says Outer Banks Dork, 'cause that's really what you are."

"Dad, Eric is being mean again!" both girls said in unison.

"Ok boy. Enough. Let's not start the day off like this."

"Sorry papadopoulos" Eric offered up.

"I talked to Rachael last night" Jamie said changing the subject. "When I first agreed to moving down here I had forgotten about her so I wanted to talk to her about it."

"See?" Chris added. "When we talked about this briefly last night, I told you there were going to be considerations that you hadn't thought about. Your cousin being one of them. What did she have to say?"

"At first she didn't know what to say. She knows how much we love it down here and even though she would miss all of us she thinks we should move here. She said, that way she could spend the summers with us."

"Yes, she could do that, provided Uncle Andy was ok with it." Chris knew that Andy would be since he also was trying to balance the single dad thing after Sue's passing. That would allow Andy three months to be just a person again, not just be a single dad. To do things that he wanted to do.

"Anyone else have any thoughts from our talk last night?" Chris asked.

Eric sheepishly said "well, I was looking forward to this swim season. After losing pretty much all my races last year because I was the youngest, I was really looking forward to being one of the oldest and win some races."

"Tell you what boy" Chris said, "While we're out today, why don't we stop by the Y to check into their swim teams." 'I also know there's a good little league down here, Mr. JW's son plays in it."

Eric responded as usual with as few words as was needed, "OK cool."

Grandma Pat chimed into the conversation. "How about you Savannah? Do you have anything to say about moving here?"

"Just one grandma. I'm real excited about daddy working for Radio Disney."

With that everyone laughed and continued onto Poor Richards, Chris's favorite breakfast spot on the Manteo Waterfront. They have the best sweet potato biscuits he would always say.

After they've all eaten and the bill was paid, they left. Grandma Pat didn't feel much like going souvenir shopping so she pulled her umbrella out of her purse and despite the rain, walked the block back home. As they parted ways, Chris said to his mom "I told Jennifer that we'd stop by Arnold's again before we left. Can you call her and make a reservation for all of us for dinner tonight?"

"Sure. In fact, I'll stop by her house on my way home to let her know."

With that Chris and the kids made off for the beach. There were mega gift shops that dot the 158 bypass all the way from Whalebone Junction in Nags Head up to the Kitty Hawk - Southern Shores line, and even though they pretty much had the exact same things to sell, Chris was pretty much counting on the kids wanting to visit each and every one. And visit them they did, including even some of the smaller ones that were already open despite not quite yet being tourist season.

After about four hours of walking up and down aisles looking at over-priced junk, the young family took a break for lunch. They stopped at Chris's former hangout when he lived down here; Sooey's BBQ in Nags Head. "They have the best pulled pork BBQ in the world," he told his kids.

"BBQ is boring" Eric said. "I'm getting the gator tail."

"Dad! Eric is gonna eat an alligator!" Savannah exclaimed. "I don't want an alligator on our table!"

"It's ok sweetheart. It's the tail, not the whole alligator. It will look just like chicken nuggets, I promise."

"Does that mean when we go to McDonald's, daddy, and you get us Chicken Nuggets, we're eating alligator?"

"No pumpkin, it's chicken. But the alligator tail looks just like that when they cook it."

"Ok, Eric, you can have the gator tail, but you're gross!" Savannah exclaimed.

Chris ordered his East Carolina style BBQ and a Red Stripe, Jamie got the chicken fingers and Savannah the mac and cheese. And as they always did when going out to dinner, the three kids ordered a Shirley Temple. It made them feel older and more sophisticated.

Once lunch was finished Eric had a question. "That was great pops, but what's for dinner?"

"I told Miss Jennifer that we'd stop by Arnold's again before we leave so we'll have dinner there. We'll take grandma out."

"Cool, I may just have me some more alligator tonight." Eric said, thinking he was cool.

Jamie added "I was hoping we would see her and Storm again. I like them a lot."

"Well, not sure we'll see Storm or Miss Jennifer. I'm not sure if they're working or not. But I promise we'll see them again before we leave."

"Daddy, can I tell them we're moving here and you're going to make the radio station Radio Disney?" asked Savannah.

"Sweetheart, first, I'm not sure moving is the right thing for us or not. We still have to think about that and talk about it some more. I want to make sure you guys weigh everything before we make a decision.

And we'll make that decision as a family. And if we do, I don't think the radio station is going to change to Radio Disney."

"You mean they don't like that idea daddy?"

"I don't think they want to do that Savannah."

"But then why are we moving here then?"

Eric getting impatient with his little sister added "hey pops just said we don't know if we're moving down here yet and if we do then he's going to be on the radio. If they have Radio Disney down here then he wouldn't have a job and we couldn't move here then." "Now be quiet and let's go find your Outer Banks Dork shirt."

"For a big brother, you're mean," Savannah pouted.

"For a little brother he's mean too," Jamie added.

"And for sisters, you're both dumb." Eric responded.

"Alright kids, knock it off or we'll just go back to grandma's and not do anymore souvenir shopping."

At the end of the shopping day, the kids all seemed satisfied with their purchases. Savannah was able to find her Outer Banks Princess shirt. Eric found a remote controlled Jeep that he could run on the sand of the beach and Jamie got a hermit crab, hermit crab food and a hermit crab case. By this time the rain had subsided and the sun started to peek through, Chris said to the kids, "how about when we get back to grandma's we swim in the pool for a bit before heading down to Arnold's for dinner?"

"Yeah" they all answered. It was Eric who then asked "Hey pops, if we don't move down here, can we get a salt water pool in our backyard like grandma's?"

"Just settle down there boy, there are a lot of things already on our plate that we have to figure out. Let's not add anything more to it."

The brood returned to grandma Pat's and changed into their bathing suits and headed down the elevator to the pool. Of course arguing as to who was going to press the button to operate the elevator. Eric won that battle, much to the consternation of his two sisters. Chris didn't change, but rather just sat in one of the Adirondack Chairs on the pool deck and watched as the kids splashed around and had some fun. Though a happy moment, Chris still had melancholy thoughts because Linda was not there to be able to enjoy this family time with them. After about an hour grandma Pat shouted down that the kids should get dried off and into some clothes. The dinner reservation was in a half hour. So they all piled into the elevator and this time Jamie pushed the button while Chris took the stairs up to the main level. As the kids went to the bedrooms to change; the girls in theirs and Eric in his dad's, grandma Pat grabbed a Red Stripe out of the refrigerator and gave to her son and said "I hope you don't mind, but when I stopped by Jennifer's this morning to make the reservation she said that she and Storm were both off so I invited them along with us."

"Not a problem for me" Chris said. "When I saw in her the pool the other morning swimming she told me to stop by for dinner, it was on her." "So happy to have along the person paying the bill."

As Chris was finishing the last of his beer, Jamie came running down the stairs. "I just looked out the window and saw Storm down the street, is it ok if I run out and say hi to her dad?"

"No need to Jamie. I just heard that she and her mother were having dinner with us tonight." "She's probably on her way here now."

"They are dad?" "That's awesome, I really like them."

"So you've said baby girl" Chris replied.

Just then the front door opened and in came both Storm and Jennifer. On the Outer Banks, neighbors are good enough friends that knocking is just a voluntary thing. Walking into someone else's house is perfectly acceptable. Storm was dressed in a Manteo High School t-shirt and jeans and Jennifer in a bright yellow sundress, both ready for dinner.

Grandma Pat grabbed her purse and despite the fact the restaurant was nearly a half mile a way they all decided to walk rather than take 2 cars. Well, it was the adults who made that decision. The kids whined the whole way about having to walk. Storm grabbed Savannah's hand and walked with Jamie on the other side of her. Eric hung with Chris, and Jennifer and grandma Pat bringing up the rear. Each group just chatted amongst themselves for the 15 minute walk.

Once they arrived at Arnold's, Jennifer led everyone to the back banquet room that she had set up earlier in the day. The table was set for all seven with a bottle of red wine already on the table for the adults and four Shirley Temples ready to go for the kids.

"Remember, you said you were picking up the tab" Chris said laughing as they entered the room.

Grandma Pat shot him a glare, much like the ones she used to give him when he was a young boy and did something that she didn't approve of. "I didn't raise you to become a cheap SOB" she said.

"Grandma, what's a SOB?" Savannah wanted to know. Must have been funny she thought, because all the adults laughed.

"Pat don't worry" Jennifer said. "I did tell Chris to come on out before they left and that I would take care of the check."

"That still doesn't excuse his boorish behavior" replied the embarrassed grandma Pat.

They all sat down. Storm between the Jamie and Savannah, then Chris, Eric, Jennifer and grandma Pat. They ordered some appetizers to share; onion rings for the kids and calamari for the adults. As Chris poured the wine he said to Jennifer, "why in the world would you want to come here on your night off to eat?" "I imagine you eat this food all the time."

"We do" chimed in Storm.

Jennifer looked to her daughter and gave her a "don't interrupt the adult conversation" type of looks. "We do Chris, but tonight I have a special menu planned. Not something that we normally serve here at Arnold's. Besides, I didn't want to pass up having dinner with your mother and her very delightful grandchildren."

"Ha burn pops!" Eric yelled out. "She wants to have dinner with us and grandma, not you!"

"That's not what I meant Eric" Jennifer explained. "I meant I wouldn't miss the chance to have dinner with all of you." "Ya'll have a very wonderful family."

As the chit chat turned to more mundane neighborhood type things; like the Meekins down the street, leaving to go visit their grandchildren in Florida next week and Martha next door having her niece coming to stay a few days from Virginia, the appetizers were delivered along with the limited dinner menu that Jennifer supplied for tonight's get together. Chris perusing the menu was very impressed. "Wow, you've pulled out all the stops here tonight. Whole Main Lobster, Filet Mignon, fresh swordfish and tuna. But I'll bet you'll never guess what I'm going to choose."

"Yes I do" said Jennifer. "That's why it's on tonight's menu. Your mother told me that you love East Carolina Pulled Pork more than anything, and it just so happens we have been getting one ready since 7 this morning."

"So you won't be offended if I have that then?" Chris asked.

"Heck no" Jennifer said. "That's what I'm having too. I was just hoping I wasn't going to be the only one. Besides, if I'm picking up the tab, it's cheaper than the filet or fresh fish" Jennifer added jokingly.

"You two can have the pulled pork, but I think I'm going to have the swordfish, grilled" said grandma Pat. "Kids what are you all having?"

Eric answered first. "I'm having gator tail again."

"Yep" Jennifer said, your grandmother told me that is what you'd want too."

"She probably told you that I like spaghetti and meatballs, didn't she?" Savannah wanted to know. "That's probably why it's on the menu."

Eric snipped at his sister "How do you know it's on the menu. You can't read dork!"

"Storm told me it was. She read it for me. And daddy, will you tell Eric to stop calling me a dork?"

"Eric!"

"Yes Savannah. That's why it's on there. Your grandmother told me it was your favorite" said Jennifer as she tried to break the tension between the little girl and her brother. "And Jamie, grandma didn't tell me your favorite, but Storm said she knew you loved Fettuccini Alfredo." "I hope she was right."

"She was right, Miss Jennifer. Thank you." "And thanks Storm for remembering."

"Sure kid." "You're like the little sister I never had." With that Jamie sat up straight at the table and beamed from ear-to-ear. She thought it cool that an older girl wanted to hang out with her.

Noticing that Chris had been left out of the chit chat that she and grandma Pat had been engaged in, Jennifer asked Chris how the trip was going.

"It's been great. Saw some old friends. Dropped by the old job."

"Old job may turn into a new job" grandma Pat added.

Jennifer looked a little confused and said "I'm not sure I follow."

Grandma Pat took it upon herself to fill in the blanks. "You know John Clark, right?"

"Yeah."

"Remember, we set it up so John had the table next to us on Chris and the kid's first day down?" "Well," grandma Pat continued, "John casually mentioned that he wanted to talk to Chris about something and to call him before leaving. Chris didn't think much of it assuming that John just needed girl advice again. Like Chris knows enough about women to be able to dispense advice, but I digress. John had approached me a few weeks ago and asked if I thought Chris would move back down here to take a job at the radio station again. I promised John that I would help with the kids so he would have no reason to say no. Chris went to visit John at the station yesterday, offered him a job and well, here we are." "Did I miss anything son?"

"No, I think you got it pretty well covered ma."

Storm all excited at hearing the news shrieked "Ya'll are gonna move here? That is so cool! I can help with babysitting if you need me!"

Chris feeling very much in a corner at this point was very cautious in his words; "we have an offer. I have no idea if it's wise for us to move here or not. That is something that we will discuss AND decide as a family."

The servers brought the two families their food. As the plates were set down in front of each and they began to dig in, grandma Pat was the one who said the obvious, "seems to me, right now it's 3-1 on moving down."

"Are you assuming I'm the dissenting vote mother?" Chris asked, "because I'm not. Let's just say three for and one not sure."

"Big decision for sure. I know what it took for me to bite the bullet to move just me and Storm down here from Richmond. At least you have a safety net with your mother here. You also have a lot of other friends that I'm sure would help. I, for one would be thrilled if ya'll moved here." "I think Storm would be too."

"I'd really rather not talk about it the rest of the evening, if you don't mind" Chris said. "Not to be a jerk, it's just that I need a break from the whole idea right now."

"No worries" grandma Pat answered, changing the subject, "so Storm how has freshman year at Manteo High School been?"

"Except for the football team losing to Currituck this year, it' been pretty good. Scary at first, but good now."

Chris, who used to be the play-by-play voice of the Manteo High School football Redskins on his first stint on Ocean 105 asked Storm if the station still broadcast the games.

"Yep, sure do. Uncle Danny Daniels does the games."

Chris thought, "hmmmm, another check for the pro side of moving here…."

The group finished up dinner and the kids each ordered a bowl of ice cream for dessert, while the adults ordered another bottle of wine for theirs. This one's on Chris, he insisted. After the dinner and dessert was consumed, Jennifer checked on a few tables in the dining room and the group began their walk back home. Once back at grandma Pat's the kids all decided to change back into their wet swim suits to hit the pool; Storm ran home and got hers. The adults sat around the pool deck watching. Chris, looking at his smart phone, sighed and said "expecting snow on Sunday back home. Looks significant. We're probably going to have to leave a day early to beat the storm."

"Well, that's no good" Jennifer offered. I couldn't imagine having to live my life around snow storms."

"Yeah, but you do have those pesky things called hurricanes that I don't have to worry about." Chris countered.

"Touché."

Grandma Pat, always one to retire to her bed early to read before going to sleep, excused herself and did just that, leaving Chris and Jennifer to close up the pool once the kids were finished. "No hurry" she said. "You all stay out here as late as you'd like and enjoy yourself. There's pop for the kids and beer and wine for anyone who wants it." "Jennifer, thank you so much for dinner. It was fabulous!"

"It was my pleasure Pat" Jennifer answered. "You have a lovely family."

And with that, grandma Pat said good night to the kids and went upstairs to the main level and her bedroom.

The kids played tag in the water, Eric always the strongest swimmer, always seeming never to be "it." Jennifer and Chris chatted. Jennifer mentioned having gone to school at the University of Virginia to study Culinary Arts. "With a father in the restaurant business, and me working in his kitchens at a very young age, I guess it was pre-ordained that would be the path I would also take."

She had a love/hate relationship with the business. She loved the business itself, the people, the challenge of turning a profit every month and the creativity involved in both menu planning and cooking. What she didn't like were the hours involved. "Honestly" she said, "if Storm didn't work with me in the restaurant, I'm not sure when or if I would ever see her." "I'm doing my best to sway her from following in the family business. I want her to do something she loves and has a passion for, and not do something because she feels obligated to follow both me and her grandfather."

"Does she seem like she wants to go in that direction now?" Chris asked.

"I don't know. I don't think so. At least she hasn't shown the self-motivation to be at the restaurant that I had at her age." "She likes performing and is trying out for the Lost Colony this summer."

The Lost Colony is a play based on the accounts of Sir Walter Raleigh's attempts to create a new world on Roanoke Island back in 1587. The play has been performed just down the street nightly in the summers since 1937. It's the longest running outdoor drama in the country.

"That's interesting" Chris said. "I always wanted to do something with the Lost Colony, but I never had the guts. Props to her for putting herself out there."

"Never had the guts?" "From what I hear you were the man in radio back in the day, and still are up in Ohio. How could you not have the guts?"

"Well it's one thing to be an idiot in a small room by yourself with a microphone in front of you. It's another to do it in front of hundreds of people with all eyes upon you." "Yeah, good for her. She's a brave little girl."

"Tell me about you." Jennifer said. "I already know from your mother the tragedies that you and the kids have gone through the last couple of years, but tell me about how you got into radio."

"Pretty boring story. You sure you want to hear it?"

"I do."

"Ok, but let me grab us a couple of beers first. Red Stripe ok?"

"Yeah. Red Stripe is one of my favorites."

As they settled back into their Adirondack chairs on the pool deck, Chris started his story on getting into radio.

"When I was a kid, like most, I wanted to be a bunch of different things. I had no inclination to follow in my father's footsteps because he was a factory worker. What I wanted to do was become, in this order, a pro football player, in fact I still do. Then I wanted to become a veterinarian, and then because my favorite show on tv at the time was The Bob Newhart Show, I wanted to become a psychologist. Then I got to high school and my Aunt Lou Ann, who was my dad's sister married my Uncle Rick. They were only 4 years older than me, so they were more like an older sister and brother than they were an aunt and uncle. Rick, at the time, worked for a radio station in Cleveland. I lived on the east side and went to a private all-boys Catholic high school on the west side, so I had to cross through downtown on my way to and from school. My uncle's radio station was downtown, so after school I would start hanging out there. The DJ on the air at the time was a guy by the name of Scott West. Scott used to let me sit in the studio with him while he was on the air to watch and listen. I remember taking notes on what Scott did. He let me press some buttons and pick out music. I had been bitten by the radio bug. I would sit at home with my little record player and practice announcing songs and time out my talking so I would be done when the lyrics began. I know, kind of a dork…"

"No, not at all. This isn't boring, it's interesting actually."

"Really?"

"Yeah, it is. Go on."

"Well, I continued hanging out in the radio station everyday for four years. Then it was time for college. I went to THEE Ohio State University to study Radio/TV. Unfortunately, I studied beer and girls instead. Going to an all-boys Catholic high school will do that to you. I got to college and was amazed that no one cared if I showed up for class or not, or did the homework or not. I had been given too much freedom at one time and couldn't handle it. My mother yanked me out of college because I was just wasting their money. And I was. I went to a broadcasting school instead. Halfway through that program an on-air, overnight spot opened up at my uncle's radio station and I decided to apply for it. He wasn't still at the big station in downtown Cleveland, he was actually now the program director at a little Adult Contemporary station in the islands of Lake Erie. So I began my radio career at WOSE 93.5 FM."

"That's pretty cool" Jennifer replied. "How did you find your way to the Outer Banks?"

"Well, I always wanted to move here" Chris continued, "the how I got here was because I got so sick of the snow and the cold." "At WOSE, I was working overnights. There was a woman on the air before me that worked from 6 to midnight. Her husband also worked at the station, he was on the air from 10am to 2pm. They only had the one car so he would drop her off at work and then come back at midnight to pick her back up. There was this one night where we were expecting a huge winter storm. Alex, the 10am to 2 guy came in about 10pm that night to get some recording work out of the way. Commercials, promos, that kind of thing. He got to the station just as the storm hit. Two hours later at midnight it had already snowed so badly that they were snowed in at the radio station with me. The three of us were stuck there for three days keeping the radio station on the air. We actually had to break into the vending machine to have food to eat. We took turns sleeping in the news director's office on the floor which was just carpet over a cement slab. It was freakin' freezing.

The Sheriff's Department had put a ban on driving throughout the county so no one was able to make it in to relieve us for three days. I think it was around hour 60 of the blizzard that I decided that was going to be my last winter in Ohio. First thing I did after that was apply for a job at Ocean 105. They gave me one and the rest is history."

"Nice job outta you. You said no more Ohio winters and where are you now?" Jennifer playfully asked. "Oh yeah, Ohio. And you have to what, cut your trip early because of snow?"

Chris sheepishly looked down and mumbled "yeah, a lot in my life hasn't exactly gone to plan lately." With that, he gulped down the last of his beer and asked Jennifer if she'd like another.

"No, but thanks. I better get Storm home. We have to work tomorrow, and I have to be there early. Big delivery coming in."

"C'mon Storm, time to dry off and hit the road youngun." Jennifer called out to her daughter.

"You guys too" Chris added. "It's been a long day, time to get some rest."

"Dad, will we get to see Storm again before leaving?" Asked the littlest, Savannah.

"Sure, we'll make sure we do. Now go get your towel. Boy, hit the power button to put the cover back on the pool."

"You got it papadopoulos" Eric yelled out.

With that, the two families said good night to each other. Each promising to see each other again before the one has to head back to Ohio and reality.

Not that living and working on the Outer Banks isn't reality too. It's just a different kind. A more enjoyable, laid back kind of reality. The kind that deep down Chris knew he was missing in his life. Since Linda died, life has been one big blur. Chris had often thought to himself that he would like life to just stop for like six months, just so he can catch back up with it again.

Chris was starting to wonder exactly why he wasn't jumping at John's job offer. It's beginning to seem like a no-brainer type of decision. Back in Ohio, Chris and the kids are pretty much left to their own devices, but here, they would have the support of his mother and his friends. The needle was starting to move in Chris's mind, towards coming back to the the Outer Banks. He still wasn't quite there yet.

After tucking the kids each in for the night it was Jamie that asked what was on everyone's minds; "Dad, are we moving here?"

"Do you all want to?" Chris asked back.

Without nary a hesitation at all, all three kids in unison yelled back with a resounding "yes!"

"Maybe." That was all the commitment that Chris could muster at the moment. "I'll tell you what, we have a long 10 hour drive home the day after tomorrow. We can talk about it then."

"Day after tomorrow?" Eric yelled out. "You mean we're leaving a day early?"

"Yeah, I looked at the weather" Chris replied, "there's a big snow storm that's going to hit on Sunday. I want to be home before it hits. I don't want to have to be driving in it."

"Another reason to move back here." Jamie said, "no more snow. Ugh."

"Yeah, but then that means no more snow days at school either." Chris added. With that he turned off the light and retired to his bedroom.

CHAPTER 10.

It was another fitful night sleep for Chris as he awoke to their last day on the Outer Banks. The kids and grandma Pat were already awake. That never happens. Chris never sleeps past the time the kids get up. At least he hadn't since Linda died. He had a sixth sense on knowing when someone was awake and he'd wake up too. Regardless of how much or how little sleep he got.

He made his way downstairs for coffee as his mother and children were about to leave. "Saves us from having to write you a note Sleepy Beauty" was the welcome he had received from his mother. "The kids and I are off for the Nags Head pier. We're having breakfast outside in the fresh air. You're not invited. This is the last day with my grandchildren before you all pull up stakes for Ohio, so I'm not sharing them today."

"Ok" was the only answer Chris came up with. "Ya'll have fun."

"We will daddy." Savannah said. "Grandma Pat is going to show me the house that you and Mommy lived in."

"And me!" Jamie yelled out.

"Oops" Savannah continued, "the house that you mommy and Jamie all lived in."

Chris, happy that he didn't have to take them there and possibly open old wounds, kissed his youngest on the forehead and said "that's good princess. You be good for grandma."

"I'm always good daddy. You better tell Eric to be good though." "He's the bad one."

"You heard her Eric." "You be good for your grandmother" Chris said as they all walked out the door.

With the day to himself, Chris didn't know where to begin. A swim in the pool? A bike ride down to the historic Ft Raleigh? Breakfast in town? He wasn't used to just having to occupy his own time. Seems much more difficult than having his day planned out by kids activities all day.

Chris got himself cleaned up in the outdoor shower and changed into a pair of clean cargo shorts and a Coastal Edge Surf Shop t-shirt and flip flops. He remembered back to the days when this was how he dressed going to work each day. He got into his car and pointed it south. He had no plan in mind. He was just going to see where the day may bring him. As he came around the corner he saw Jennifer outside at Arnold's unloading a delivery truck. She looked to be alone, so he stopped and offered to help.

"This is how you want to spend your last day on the Outer Banks?" "Unloading sacks of potatoes and onions from the back of a delivery truck?" She asked.

"Potatoes and Onions?" I was hoping it was a beer delivery I was gonna help you with." "Oh well, too late to back out now."

"Careful" Jennifer continued. "You're already becoming an Outer Banker again."

"How's that?" Chris asked.

"Neighbor helping neighbor. That's how we do it down here."

That is exactly how they do it down here, Chris thought. Neighbor helping neighbor. Not a lot of that going on back in Ohio. People are in too much of a hurry to take the time to help each other out.

Jennifer interrupted his thought with a "Hey! Lift from your legs, not your back! There's going to be no worker's comp claim here old man!"

Chris laughed and went back to work finishing up the unloading. Once done, Jennifer said "well you helped me cut that job in half. We have time for a cup of coffee before my next delivery."

"Coffee sounds great to me. Thanks." Chris answered.

Jennifer went back in the kitchen and grabbed 2 large mugs filled to the rim with piping hot coffee. She sat one down in front of Chris and asked "any more thoughts as to what you and the kids are going to do?"

"I don't know what the right thing is" Chris said. "There's so much to consider. The cost of living is high at the beach. I'll be making less money. For the most part the kids are settled into a life without their mother. I don't know if adding another upheaval is what's best."

"Sounds to me" Jennifer said, "that you already have your mind made up."

"Yeah maybe." The two then finished their coffee in silence, and as they did so, the next delivery truck made it's way to the back kitchen door.

"Well, back to work for me" said Jennifer. "Good luck to you and the kids. I hope it all works out for you back in Ohio. I still think the Outer Banks would be a much better place if ya'll were here."

"Yeah, thanks" Chris replied. As he made his way back to his car, he felt a sudden load on his shoulders. All this week that load seemed to have disappeared being back on the Outer Banks, but now that he pretty much decided in his mind that they were staying in Ohio, that weight had returned. He knew he had to discuss the decision with the kids at some point. After all, he did tell them and grandma Pat that this would be a family decision and not solely his. He knew it would be difficult to sway them to his position. But he was an adult, he thought, surely they'll understand I know what's best for this family.

A few minutes later, Chris found himself at the beach that he and Linda used to go to when living here. It was the same beach access at milepost 11 where the USS Huron went aground and sank in the wee morning hours back in 1877 taking 98 souls to their death. He wasn't sure how or why he steered his car here, it seemed to be through divine intervention some how. Chris got out of his car and walked down to the water's edge. With it still being very early in the tourist season, he had the entire beach to himself. As he looked to the right, he could see the Nags Head pier. He knew his mother and kids were there having their last breakfast together. With it being too far off in the distance, he couldn't see them.

Chris sat down on the sand. He sat there a good long time as images from the past came running through his brain. He was sitting very close to the exact spot of the picture he had taken years ago of Linda and their brand new yellow lab Jaxson. He recalled how Jaxson would body surf next to him as Chris shredded his own waves. He recalled how Jaxson may have even saved his life down the beach one day when the dog swam into shore and got the attention of a lifeguard when Chris got caught in a rip current.

Chris remembered the picnic dinners Linda would pack and they would eat during the late Fall afternoons when they would have this entire beach to themselves, much like Chris had now. Chris also recalled those touch football games and sand volleyball games that John Clark and Uncle Danny Daniels would organize on this very beach against the rival radio station Swampy 97.

The longer he sat there, the less that weight felt on his shoulders. It was like the memories had washed it away. Chris always said that Linda always knew the right answer and he always trusted in her. By him driving to this beach to experience the warm feelings that washed over him, was that really Linda who drove the car here and parked it? Was it her divine intervention that made it so that Chris found his way to this particular beach? Chris never a believer in such things was starting to warm up to the possibility of a guardian angel watching over him. The nuns had always talked about them during his Catholic school days. Are they really real, he thought.

Chris got up and realized he hadn't eaten anything yet today. He went down the road to Ocean 105 to visit John. Maybe I can convince him to pre-record some of his show and we can grab lunch, he thought.

Chris pulled the car into a spot in front of the radio station. The speakers on the outside of the building were playing The Beatles "Rocky Raccoon."

"Now somewhere in the Black Mountain Hills of Dakota, there lived a young boy named Rocky Raccoon...."

John was the local Fab 4 guru and it wasn't a surprise they were playing when he arrived. Chris entered the building and was greeted warmly by Annie, "John mentioned you might be dropping by again" she said. "You can just go right in the studio."

The song had ended and John was explaining to his listening audience some trivia about the song Rocky Raccoon so Chris waited for the "ON-AIR" light to go out. Once it did, Chris walked into the studio.

"Bro!" John yelled out. "I was hoping you would stop in again this week."

"I'll tell you what John, you have made this week a difficult one for me."

John seemed surprised by this and said "Why? It's you that always says that if there was ever a fish out of water, it was you in Ohio. I would have thought this was a no-brainer for you."

"If it were just me by myself, yeah it would have been." "But now I have three other people to consider in all my decisions." "Any chance you can bug out early and we can go grab some lunch so we can chat?"

"I think we can arrange that, you know, providing it's not to give me bad news."

"Honestly John, an hour ago, it would have been. An hour ago I told Jennifer over at Arnold's that we were going to stay put in Ohio. Now? I'm not sure which way to turn. Asking your opinion on this thing seems to be counterproductive, but you're my friend and I know you'll do your best to help guide me in the right direction."

"Ok Bro, but you know which direction I think is the right one."

"Yeah, I get that, but maybe I just need to hear that to push me in the right direction."

While John pre-recorded the last hour of his show, Chris waited for him outside. The day was brilliantly lit by the sun. Much more brilliantly than it ever seemed to shine in Ohio. Chris looked out to the Bypass just in time to see his mother's car go racing by. Judging by the direction it appeared she and the kids were heading to the Villas Condos. The condo development that Chris, Linda and Jamie all lived in at the end of Villa Drive on the banks of the Roanoke Sound. Though he wasn't exactly champing at the bit to go himself and re-open some old wounds, he was glad the kids were able to visit.

A short time later, John came out of the radio station with his normal "ok bro. Where do you want to go?"

"Some place where I can get a crab cake sandwich and a beer" Chris replied.

"Know just the place bro."

A few minutes later, the two pulled into the parking lot at Gershe's Waterfront Grille located on the Manteo - Nags Head Causeway. Gershe's has been an Outer Banks landmark since the late 1950's. The original owner came down to the Outer Banks from New York to open an authentic New York style deli. Over the course of the years it has morphed into the best casual seafood joint in all of Dare County, now that Michael, the youngest son has taken over the day-to-day operation. Michael was working the host stand when John and Chris arrived.

Upon entering the restaurant, John approached Michael with a "Gershe bro!" No one ever called Michael, Michael. He was always just simply referred to as Gershe. "This is my buddy Chris, you might remember him from many moons ago when he did the morning show at the radio station."

"Indeed I do" Gershe replied. "Nice to see you again Chris. You too John."

"Thanks Gershe" Chris responded. I haven't been here in years. Great to be back, although I didn't realize you have the best crab cake in town. I remembered pastrami here, but not crab."

"Yeah. You have to change with the times" Gershe responded. "Give the people what they want. They don't want corned beef anymore. They want crab, clams and oysters. So that's what we give them." "Would you two like a table over looking the water?"

Looking over the busy restaurant John replied "you have one of those? Seems pretty busy to me."

"Sure we do" Gershe said. "I always keep a table on the water in reserve whenever one of our local dignitaries comes in."

"Not sure we're all that" Chris said."But we'll take it nonetheless."

"Wonderful gentlemen. Follow me this way please."

Gershe led Chris and John through the restaurant, winding their way through tables filled with patrons of all types. Businessmen entertaining clients, some county workers grabbing a quick bite, and some tourists who had decided to come down and make a long weekend of it. They got to the back corner where a table for two sat empty along the plate glass window overlooking Roanoke Sound.

"This work ok?" Gershe asked.

"This is great bro. Thanks."

Before leaving to inform the server that her table had been seated, Gershe took their drink order. Red Stripe for Chris. A Corona for John. "Very good. Your server, Kathy, will bring those over for you and get your lunch order." "Chris, nice to see you again. Now that you know we have the best crab cake in the county, perhaps you'll come visit again?" Gershe said just before walking away.

"You just might," Chris mumbled to himself. "You just might."

Just a very few minutes later, Kathy delivered the Red Stripe and the Corona to the table and took their lunch orders. Crab Cake sandwich for Chris. A Blackened Grouper sandwich for John.

"So bro, you said something that made me a little uneasy when you came in."

"Oh?"

"You said that an hour ago you would have given me bad news. Is that no longer the case?"

"John, I would be a liar if I told you I had an answer for you. I guess if you want to look at things positively, no news IS good news right?"

"I suppose so bro, but honestly, there is still time. Like I said, Uncle Danny will be in place for at least another month. I don't need an answer before you leave the beach on Sunday."

"Tomorrow. We're leaving the beach tomorrow. Big snow storm expected to hit Ohio on Sunday and I told the kids I didn't want to get caught driving in it, so we're leaving a day early."

"Bro, that sucks, but I get it. You got to be safe. You are the last parent these kids have."

"Exactly! That's why I am struggling with the answer here. I don't have room to screw up. It's just me. The kids and I only have me to depend on. That's why I have to be sure."

"You know bro, down here, it's not just you they have to depend on. They'll have your mother, and your friends JW and Bonnie. Hell, they even have their dear ol' Uncle John."

"Great. With you around, my kids will learn to call everyone bro. That's just what I need!"

With that, both John and Chris had a good laugh. It was a laugh that Chris needed. There had been so few of those lately.

At that moment, Kathy was back with the crab cake sandwich and the blackened grouper. After setting the plates down, she went back to the bar to get another round of beers for each.

Chris taking a bite of his sandwich explained "Sure beats a pastrami on rye any day of the week." "I can't get a sandwich like this back in Ohio."

"Another plus mark in the pro column for moving down bro?"

"Yeah. There's many checks in the pro column of the pro/con list that I've been keeping in my head. The problem is that all of them added together doesn't seem to outweigh that one BIG con check mark. The one that keeps nagging at me. We have a life in Ohio. The kids have their school, friends and cousin, and I have my job at the radio station.

They have been very good to me after Linda died. They've even allowed me to change shifts to accommodate me getting the kids off to school and pick them up again after. I'm just confused right now. I wish Linda were here."

John took a long look into his friends eyes. They were sad. He hadn't noticed exactly how sad they've become. Sure, he noticed they weren't as bright on that first day when they ran into each other at Arnold's, but he hadn't really noticed how uninspired they now appeared. "You have a lot on your plate bro. There's no doubt about that. Whatever you decide, you know that I'm there to support you 100%. You can always count on me."

"Thanks buddy. Just allow me to put some distance on this place before I give you my answer. Here, everything is so out of order right now. I'm not working. The kids aren't in school and doing their extra curricular activities. Let me get back home and into our normal stride, and I'll have an answer for you. Give me a week."

"You got it bro. If you want it, the job is yours. You let me know when you're ready."

"It's not a question of whether I want it. I do want it. It's more a question of whether it's the right move for the family."

Lunch was finished up with the conversation drifting to the more mundane. The Cleveland Browns, and their lack of ability to win, the new Hardee's going in on Roanoke Island and to John's latest girl problem. The two said their goodbyes in the parking lot, Chris promising to get John his answer by this time next week. John, in his mind figuring he better start thinking of a plan B. As they each got into their cars John yelled out "hey bro, all the answers you're looking for; they're right here on this beach. Deep down you know it, but you're just too close to the situation to see it. I hope our chat next week goes well."

"Me too John" Chris yelled out, and to himself, Chris mumbled. "Me too." And with that, both guys were off to their separate locations. John, back to the radio station; Chris back to his mother's. Chris needed a swim. A good long swim. It's how he's always been able to clear his mind.

As Chris drove past Arnold's, he noticed the parking lot was empty. The lunch rush, apparently over. Jennifer was out on the front deck in one of the rocking chairs so he pulled into the parking lot. As he plopped down in the rocking chair next to hers Jennifer said "Well hello Buckeye Chris."

"Buckeye Chris?"

"Yeah, it's my new nickname for you since you're a resident of Ohio and all."

"Yeah, about that. I spent the last several hours with John Clark. He got out of work early and we had lunch together. Best Crab Cake I ever had, by the way."

"Gershe's Waterfront Grille?"

"Yep. Anyway, John has me thinking. Going to the beach I used to go to has me thinking. That's the damn problem, everything has me thinking. I need to stop thinking about this for a while. I have this small window of a vacation here and I've wasted it being stressed."

"I agree" Jennifer said. "What you need to do is to enjoy yourself now and you can have all the time to think when you get back home. Not to mention on that ten-hour car ride tomorrow."

"Yeah, not looking forward to that exactly. Used to be Linda and I would take turns driving, now as with everything anymore, it's all on me."

"Chris, maybe it's not my place to say, but from a strictly outsider point of view, it seems to me that what you and your family needs is this move down here. Up in Ohio it is all on you, and I have a feeling it's all taking a toll. Down here, you have your mother. You have your friends. You have me and Storm to help. It wouldn't be all on you. That could be the best gift for your kids in the long run, not having a father who has this tremendous weight on his shoulders all the time."

"You know for a country girl, you make a lot of sense."

"What country girl? I'm from Richmond. The last time I looked that's a pretty big effing city!"

Both Chris and Jennifer laughed as Chris got up to leave. As he did he said to Jennifer "You know, we don't know each other all that well, but you're the one person that gave me exactly the piece of information I needed to hear. Thank you for that."

"No worries Chris. Glad I was able to drive some sense into that Yankee head of yours."

"Thanks Jennifer. I'll call you when we are back in Ohio to let you know which way I've decided to go." "Reckon I'll see you when I see you."

"You'll see me tonight. Your mom called earlier. She said the kids decided they wanted to have their last dinner here before leaving in the morning."

"Of course they do" Chris said laughing as he walked to his car. "See you tonight then."

Chris got in his car, drove to his mothers and wasn't exactly shocked to see the kids all playing in the pool. Savannah was the first to see him and shouted "Daddy, we saw the house you and mommy and Jamie lived in. It was so pretty! I like how you could see the water from it. Grandma Pat showed me the pier where you and mommy used to take Jaxson to play in the water!"

Jax had been the family pet up until about a year ago when he had died of old age. It had been a string of really bad luck when it came to things that Chris and his kids loved. First they lost their Aunt Sue, then the only dog they've ever known and then their mother.

"Did she also show you the pool there where I taught Jamie to swim?"

"Yes daddy, but there's two there. She didn't know which one it was and Jamie didn't remember."

"Next time we go I'll show you which one it was sweetheart."

"Thanks Daddy!"

Just then Eric did a cannonball off the pool deck getting everyone and everything soaking wet. "Great boy. Now I might as well go get my bathing suit on and join you guys."

"That's the idea pops. And hurry up about it!"

Chris took the elevator back up to the main level and found his mother looking at houses for sale on the internet. "Looking to sell the place ma?"

"Me?" She answered. "No. No. Just looking."

"Sure you are. Just looking."

"You heading down with the kids to the pool Chris?"

"Yeah."

"Good. Talk to them. Listen to what each is saying. I really think you need to take what each one feels into your heart. You take too much on your shoulders and don't really listen to what they're telling you."

"Mom. I appreciate what you're saying. All I have been doing is thinking about this decision. Too much maybe. I told John today that I need to get distance from this place to make the best decision possible. I think the kids need distance too. I'll have my answer by this time next week."

"By the way" grandma Pat said, "make sure you have a clean shirt. If you don't, bring one down here I'm about to do some of the kids laundry. We're having dinner at Arnold's tonight. I got us the back room again. Jennifer, Storm, JW and Bonnie, and their two kids, and John and his date will all be there since it's your last night in town."

"Yeah I heard" Chris said. "I just saw Jennifer at the restaurant just before coming here. She did mention that we were having dinner there tonight, but didn't mention that it was going to be some huge party."

Chris went upstairs to check on what clothes were clean and what needed washing. He came back down and said, "well, I do have one clean shirt left, it's Jennifer's ex-husband's baseball jersey. I reckon I shouldn't wear that one."

"Yeah, I reckon not." Grandma Pat replied.

After spending a couple of hours in the saltwater pool and in the North Carolina sun, Chris was finally able to put the decision out of his mind and just have fun with his kids. They laid on the pool rafts and took turns dumping each other off. They played tag. They squirted each other with the water cannons that grandma Pat had for the neighborhood kids to play with. This is what this vacation was supposed to be, he thought. It wasn't supposed to turn out the way it did.

Finally it was time to get out, get dried off and into the freshly laundered clothes that grandma Pat had set out for each one.

"Grandma?" Jamie asked, "will we see Storm tonight at Arnold's"

"Actually, we'll see her before that. Miss Jennifer is already there so Storm is going to ride over with us."

"Can we walk over again daddy? That was fun the last time we did that." Savannah asked.

"That's up to your grandmother" Chris answered.

"Of course we can sweetheart" grandma Pat chimed in. "Just as soon as Storm gets here, we'll leave."

They didn't have to wait long. Storm came bounding up the stairs to the house a few moments later.

Announcing her arrival was Savannah. "Yay Jamie, Storm is here!" It has often been said by Chris that Savannah has never had a thought in her life that she hadn't verbalized.

"Hi Savannah" said Storm. "You ready to go?" "You can hold both my hand and Jamie's hand as we walk over. That's if it's ok with you Mr Chris."

"Of course it is Storm."

"Good dad, 'cause Storm is like my big sister" said Savannah.

"Mine too" added Jamie.

All Eric had to say to all this was, "puke."

Chris' thoughts were a bit different. He was beginning to wonder if the girls had gotten together, with a little coaching from their grandmother perhaps, to stage this whole big sister thing for his benefit. Perhaps to sway his decision just a bit....

"Ok, if we're going to get there on time, we best be off" grandma Pat said, interrupting Chris's thoughts. "We don't want to have JW, Bonnie and their kids waiting on us."

"What about John and his date? You don't mind having them wait on us, mom?" Chris asked teasingly.

"I'm sure John and his date will be just fine. I'm sure they can entertain themselves."

The crew all made their way to Arnold's. The timing was impeccable, as they arrived just as JW's clan pulled into the lot. They all said their hellos and proceeded into the restaurant. John was already in the back room, talking about his lastest trip he had taken to the songwriting's convention in Nashville to his date, who he introduced as Ronnie.

Savannah tugging at Chris's leg, whispered in his ear "Daddy, Mr John's girlfriend has a boy's name"

"That's just a nickname sweetheart. Ronnie is short for Veronica."

"Oh, just like how yours is short for Christine?" That joke, for whatever reason always made Savannah laugh.

They each took their places as John finished up his story and introduced Ronnie to everyone. Grandma Pat, JW and Bonnie and Jennifer, of course already knew her as the broker for Ronnie Realty. Everybody knew everybody down here.

Chris leaned over and whispered into John's ear "really dude, a realtor. I'm guessing she's just going to "happen" to have a list of houses for the kids and me?"

"You got it all wrong bro. She's not here to do that. She's my honest to God date tonight. She may actually be the one bro."

"John, I've heard that sentence, let's see......six or seven times now?"

"Guilty bro."

Grandma Pat stood and proposed a toast. "To my son and his wonderful kids. They have had a very difficult year and potentially more difficult times ahead, may they find happiness and peace. To the rest of you, thank you for being there for my son. Since I've moved down here, you've all also become friends of mine. Thanks to you all!"

It was Chris's turn. Standing, he said "you all know I don't like talking in front of people...."

"Yeah right, pops. You love it" Chimed in Eric.

"But I want to say that I appreciate each and every one of you. You've all been a sounding board for me and you've welcomed me and my family into yours. Some of you," Chris continued, looking straight at John, "have even managed to make my life a bit more complicated right now. Thank you. Also, how about a big thank you to the hostess of tonight's dinner. Here's to Jennifer and the staff at Arnold's."

"Here here" everyone shouted out.

Jennifer looked at Chris and said, "if you think that's going to get you ANOTHER free meal, you sir, are sadly mistaken!"

With that the entire party laughed and Chris said "tonight is on me. Everyone have fun and relax."

With that, the two servers came around and took everyone's dinner order. Chris looked around at all the smiling faces. The laughter, the kids all playing with each other, and his heart was happy. He thought back to their lives in Ohio and it made his stomach hurt a bit. In reflecting on that life, all he saw was struggle and just trying to deal with grief and doing his best to get by. He knows coming here life would be much happier, but what nagged at him was whether he was willing to live his life happier. Would it be right? He often wondered. Chris knew what he was feeling was survivor's guilt, but he couldn't seem to get past that. Linda died. She wasn't allowed to partake in all the kid's joys. He felt like that part of him died along with her. He didn't feel like he was "allowed" to enjoy life for some reason. Moving on felt like he wasn't honoring his late wife. She wasn't allowed to move on, why should he be able to, he often thought.

Shaking him out of his deep thought was Jennifer who asked "so what time are you and the kids leaving tomorrow?"

"I want to be up and on the road before the sun comes up. It's a ten-hour drive in normal conditions, and I don't know if we'll hit the leading edge of that storm or not. I figure, better safe than sorry."

"That's too bad" Jennifer said. "I know Storm is really going to miss you guys. I will too. I truly hope that you make the decision to relocate here. I think you four would be much happier if you did, but I completely understand if you don't. Your life has already been put into an upheaval, I can't imagine what a second upheaval would be like. But anyway, whatever decision you make, I hope we can stay in touch, I know the kids plan on doing that through Facebook."

"Yeah, no doubt. We can do that. And who knows. We may even be neighbors one day. I hope to know that answer to that by this time next week."

"Good luck to you, either way." Jennifer replied cheerfully.

At that moment, the dinner was being brought in by the two servers. Everyone enjoyed the meal and the fellowship. John told radio stories; JW and Bonnie filled everyone in on the goings on back in Colington Harbour, the kids; all of them, related what they were learning in school while Chris just sat back and took it all in. Something like this just wouldn't happen in Ohio, he thought. This is a different place. A different pace. People take the time here to get to know each other. Help each other and genuinely care about each other. Each person's success is as important to the group as it is to that one specific individual. Leaving tomorrow will be hard. Not coming back to live will be even harder, but sometimes tough choices have to be made.

As dinner and dessert ended, it was time to say goodbyes to everyone. Chris and his kids needed to get up early and hit the road for Ohio. Chris actually didn't mind if the kids stayed up late, that would allow them to sleep in the car for part of their journey. But he had to get some shut eye. The final laughter was heard in the back room. The final tears of saying goodbye were shed and before to much longer it was all over. The getaway, the trip, the good times and the making of new friends in Storm and Jennifer. All there was left to do now was to go back to grandma Pat's to finish packing, load the car, and to try and get some sleep.

CHAPTER 11.

Thinking back, Chris probably hasn't had a decent night's sleep in over two years. Not since Linda's diagnosis came back, and last night was no exception. Chris spent the night tossing and turning. His mind racing with thoughts. Lots of thoughts. Thoughts about he and Linda living here. Thoughts about Jamie being born here. Thoughts about taking the job back in Ohio. Thoughts about his sister-in-law Sue dying. Thoughts about Linda dying. And now thoughts about where life was going to take both him and the kids. Would life be better on the Outer Banks for the family, or would they be better off staying in Ohio. Each side had its pros and each side had its cons. Seemingly the con side of the ledger had fewer in number, but their weight was much heavier. There would be no clear cut choice and there would be no telling if in fact the right choice was even made. Maybe years down the line the decision could be judged as either right or wrong, but by then it would be too late.

Chris rolled over, looked at the clock just as it changed to 445 am. Might as well get up and get things moving, he thought. That would get us home by dinner barring any unforeseen obstacles. So Chris dragged himself out of bed, grabbed a towel and went downstairs to the outside shower to wash the sleep off of him. The commotion of going outside must have woke his mother on the main level of the house because she was up and had the coffee going when Chris came back inside.

"I'll have a thermos ready and some food packed up for you by the time you get dressed and carry the kids to the car" grandma Pat said to her son.

"Thanks ma. I wish we didn't have to cut the trip short by a day. It's been so nice spending this time with you. We all needed the getaway. Thank you for everything."

"I'm sorry to see you go. It's been a sad night for me knowing that the house will be empty again. But I'm keeping happy thoughts that you four may soon be back. This time permanently."

"Thanks mom. You'll be the first to know of our decision."

Chris went upstairs to carry each of his children to the car. First Jamie, then Eric and finally Savannah. Grandma Pat came downstairs with Chris and Savannah to say goodbye to her family. She kissed each on the cheek, said she loved them and gently closed the car door. Chris hugged his mother, kissed her on the cheek and once again thanked her for everything. "Just so you know" he said before leaving, "I won't forget that you held out on me and didn't tell me about your conversation with John prior to me getting here."

"If that's the worst thing I did as a mother" she replied, "I did ok for myself."

"Yes you did. Love you mom."

"Love you too Christopher." With that, Chris got behind the wheel and started the car.

Chris put the car in reverse and pulled out of the driveway, leaving grandma Pat standing there alone waving. Chris put the car in drive and went down the street, down past Jennifer and Storm's house where a light was on in the kitchen.

Chris wondered if Jennifer was already up to greet the day. He drove past Arnold's, the spot where so much has happened this past week. It's where he initially ran into John who wanted to talk to him. It's where he and his kids got to know Jennifer and Storm. It's where the farewell party took place just a few short hours ago. It was sad to think that he and the kids won't be eating there again anytime soon. They wouldn't be able to play the music at the table jukeboxes, he wouldn't be able to have real authentic East Carolina pulled pork. Chris took a left onto the Manteo -Nags Head Causeway and crossed the bridge that allowed the fisherman access out of Pirate's Cove Marina and into Roanoke Sound and out to Oregon Inlet to the Gulf Stream. Shortly after crossing the bridge, Gershe's Waterfront Grille appeared on the left. Chris could taste that crab cake all over again. At Whalebone Junction, Chris decided to take the slower, yet more scenic route off the beach as he made his way to Virginia Dare Trail, or more commonly referred to as, the Beach Road. The 158 Bypass would have been faster, but Chris was in no hurry to leave Dare County as he crossed through the towns of Nags Head, Kill Devil Hills and Kitty Hawk. Soon enough Chris found himself on the bridge heading over to Point Harbor in Currituck County and back onto the mainland as he headed north for Ohio. And as he did, Chris felt a tear run down his cheek.

Chris continued the drive through Currituck County enjoying some coffee from the thermos his mother had made while the kids continued to sleep in the backseat. His intention was to stop somewhere around Richmond, Virginia. That would put it at around 830 in the morning and approximately seven hours from home.

The drive through North Carolina's Currituck County was monotonous as towns clicked on by. Harbinger, Grandy, Javisburg, Moyock and then finally the state line line and into Chesapeake, Virginia. Crossing the bridge over the Chesapeake Bay before disappearing in the tunnel below it, Chris took a last, long look at the water.

He knew this was the last he would see of it the rest of the way home as they proceeded both north and further inland to the west.

With the radio off as to not disturb the kids while they slept, Chris spent several hours inside his head as the trip proceeded thorough Southeastern Virginia. Past Hampton, Newport News and Williamsburg. Chris remembered the time that he and Linda spent the day in Colonial Williamsburg. It was right after they were married, they couldn't afford a honeymoon so they came here for the day. They spent time walking the tourist sites and through the campus of William & Mary College. Chris being a history buff thought it would be cool if one his kids went to school there, as did the son of George Washington, once upon a time. No time for stopping today, there was a snow storm to beat so Chris kept driving.

In the 45 minutes between Williamsburg and Richmond the kids started waking up, one by one. First Savannah, then Eric and finally Jamie. Jamie was the sleeper of the three. From the day Chris and Linda brought her home from Albamarle Hospital in Elizabeth City after she was born, Jamie slept through the night. And the morning and through most of the afternoon, if she was allowed. One thing Jamie knew how to do, and that was sleep.

"Daddy, are we almost home?" Savannah sleepily said.

"Does this look like home dork?" Eric answered for his father.

"Dad! Eric is being mean again!"

"Ok, kids. Come on, we've got a long way to go yet. Let's not start arguing now." Chris pleaded. "Who's hungry?"

"Me daddy!" Savannah replied.

"Me too" Eric added.

"I'm tired' said Jamie as she let out a huge yawn.

"There's a really good diner on the west side of Richmond coming up in about a half hour. Your mother and I would stop there whenever we would drive back to Ohio. We could stop there for breakfast."

"Have I been there dad?" Asked Jamie.

"Yes, likely you have been daughter number one" Chris answered.

"Hahaha, you're daughter number two Eric." Joked Savannah.

"That didn't even make sense dork" Eric replied. "If you're going to try and burn me, you'll have to do better than that."

"All right kids, that's enough." Chris said as he turned on the radio, hoping that would be the distraction they needed to keep from arguing.

"Radio Disney daddy!" Savannah yelled out.

"If I can find it, I will pumpkin."

Chris scanned all the stations but couldn't find the Radio Disney option outside of Richmond. He stopped the radio at a Top 40 station. He didn't particularly care for the music, but the kids seemed to. Chris followed the signs for I-64 West and soon came upon the exit for the diner. Chris and the kids piled out of the car for some breakfast.

As they were being sat at their table Chris said, "Remember kids, let's make this fast so we can get back on the road and get home before the snow"

"Ok daddy" said Savannah. "I think I'll get the kid's silver dollar pancakes."

"Sounds like a plan" said Chris. "You two know what you want?" He asked Eric and Jamie.

"I'll get the silver dollar pancakes too" added Eric.

"Me too" said Jamie, still yawning."

Knowing this was his last chance to get some authentic southern food for a little while, Chris ordered for himself the sausage gravy and biscuits.

"How far are we from home daddy?" Savannah asked.

"Oh, about 7 hours or so." Chris answered.

"How long is that daddy?" Savannah wanted to know.

Trying to figure a way to explain what 7 hours was to his youngest, Chris answered "well sweetie, it's about 4 Little Mermaids."

"What do you mean daddy?" Savannah asked, confused.

"What he means is if you watch the Little Mermaid 4 times, then we'll be home." Eric answered for his father.

"Thanks boy."

"No worries papadopoulos." Eric answered.

"Can I watch the Little Mermaid DVD when we get back in the car? I'll watch it 4 times and time you daddy."

"Sure sweetheart" Chris answered.

"Just make sure you put on your headphones so I don't have to hear it" Eric said to his little sister.

With that, breakfast was served. The young family ate their food quickly before making a stop in the restroom.

"Jamie, take your little sister in and stay with her please. I'll wait outside the door for you two." Chris said. It was always times like this he felt the most awkward. He couldn't take Savannah into the mens room; she was too old for that. But at the same time, he always felt uneasy letting the two girls go in by themselves, especially in a strange place. You never know the type of people may be hanging around wanting to cause a problem. Chris waited outside the door of the ladies room until the girls finished up. He then put them in the car and locked the door. He and Eric went back inside to the men's room. When they returned to the car, Chris had noticed that Jamie had already gotten the Little Mermaid playing on Savannah's DVD player, and her headphones on. Despite only being early into her teenage years, Jamie had already begun the duties of being a surrogate mother to her little sister. A thought that both warmed Chris and made him sad. He didn't want Jamie to feel like she had to be Savannah's mother. He just wanted Jamie to be a typical teenager and not have to worry about such things.

Chris started the engine and steered the car back to I-64 west and home. As he got on the road he looked in his rear view mirror at the kids. Jamie and Savannah were watching the movie while sharing headphones. Eric was playing one of his video games so Chris turned the radio to a classic rock station and settled into the drive. About a hour later they were passing the exit for Charlottesville, the home of the University of Virginia, the school that Thomas Jefferson founded when Chris's phone rang. "Hi mom," he said.

"Hi Chris. Everything alright?"

"So far, so good. We just had breakfast and we're back on the road. We're in Charlottesville now."

"Jennifer came over this morning before going to work. She said she had the weather channel on and noticed that the snow that you guys are expecting is coming a little earlier than expected and the line of the storm has drifted south. it looks like you'll hit it somewhere between Beckley and Charleston, West Virginia."

"Oh that's just great" Chris said exasperated. "That is the one part of the drive I hate already."

The stretch of I-77 between Beckley and Charleston is a challenging drive, even in good conditions. It's approximately 50 miles of twisting, turning road in the mountains. It's a stretch that is heavily populated by semi-trucks that scream down the mountains and chug back up the other side. Chris didn't like driving it at all, let alone in snow. The road is no doubt going to be treacherous.

"Well, keep plugging away" his mother said. "Worst case scenario you guys have to pull off and get a hotel somewhere."

"I guess" Chris said sighing. "But if we do that, then we're likely to be stranded there for a couple or three days." "I'll keep driving as long as it's safe."

"Ok son" Grandma Pat said. "I'll keep an eye on the weather channel and let you know of any other news."

"Thanks ma."

"Ok. You be careful" Grandma Pat said, "you're carrying precious cargo."

"Will do." And with that, Chris eased down on the gas and sped up an additional 10 miles per hour, hoping the faster speed will get them through that stretch of highway before the storm. Surely, he thought, if we got stopped by highway patrol, they'll understand and let me off with a warning.

Chris' earlier thoughts of the big decision he had to make were now replaced by the thoughts of driving through the impending storm. We should have left even earlier, he thought, early enough to not have to worry about this. Or we should have left later. We could have stayed on the Outer Banks an additional three or four days and let the storm play out before making for home. But this is where they were and all Chris could do now was deal with it. The next two and a half hours of driving will be a race against time….and snow.

More towns clicked on by; Waynesboro, Staunton, Lexington, Virginia. Just before getting to Covington, Virginia, Savannah, from the back seat called out, "daddy, one Little Mermaid is over. Just 3 more to go, then we're home."

"That's great" Chris said, as he looked at his daughter in the rear view mirror.

"Daddy, I will let you know when this one is done too, so you know there's only 2 more to go."

"Thanks sweetie. That is very helpful."

White Sulpher Springs and Lewisburg, West Virginia were the next two towns to come and go. Up ahead, on I-64, snow clouds appeared ominous in the early afternoon sky. Chris glanced at the clock on the car's dashboard. 12:45, less than an hour to Beckley. Chris' plan was to stop in Beckley for lunch, but now that was out of the question. They would have to go to a McDonalds drive-thru when they stopped at the Harper Rd exit for gas and get right back on the road.

Light snow was starting to fall as Chris turned the car in a more northerly direction as he merged onto I-77 towards Charleston. This was the stretch of the highway where I-64 and I-77 ran as the same interstate. "Just hold off for another hour please" Chris mumbled to himself. "Let me get 50 more miles up the road and then I will deal with whatever weather is thrown at me."

From the backseat Chris heard Eric say "hey papadopoulos, we're getting hungry back here. Can we stop for lunch?"

"Yeah boy. We're going to stop for gas here in about 15 minutes or so. We can run through the drive thru at McDonalds. Do me a favor and ask your sisters what they want. I want to just keep moving."

"You got it pops." Eric took his sister's orders and was ready once Chris pulled the car into McDonalds. "Two Chicken McNugget Happy Meals with Orange drinks and a quarter pounder meal for me with a Coke please." Chris also ordered two cheeseburgers and a small fry for himself along with a large coffee. Once the food was distributed to the kids, Chris pulled across the street to the BP station and filled up the car with gas, and back onto I-77 they went.

In the 15 minutes it took to get food and put gas in the car, the snow started falling heavier. It hadn't started accumulating yet, but it had turned dark as night and the snow was coming straight at him making it very hard to see. Once leaving Charlottesville Chris had been averaging approximately 80 miles an hour. He was now down to a crawl. A quick glance down at the speedometer told Chris that he was down to 35 miles per hour. He reached over to the dashboard and flipped on the hazard lights. Ten more minutes up the road and the speed was now down to approximately 20 miles an hour as the highway became slick with slushy snow. About two inches had fallen already. Semi's on the road in both lanes made it difficult to try and pass, not that he would have wanted to anyway. The ups and downs of the roads, the twists and the turns made for plenty of white knuckle driving.

"Daddy. Two Little Mermaids are done. Only two more to go!" Exclaimed Savannah excitedly.

"Thanks pumpkin. But this snow has slowed us down. It's going to take us more than just two more."

"How many more daddy? I want to be home now."

Eric butted in, "Savannah, can't you tell that pops is having a hard time with the snow and the traffic?" "Leave him alone if you want us to get home in one piece!"

"Daddy, Eric is being mean again."

Quickly losing his patience, not at the kids, but at their present situation Chris answered "please kids. No more arguing. I need to concentrate on the road right now."

Jamie, trying to help out her dad tried to divert Savannah's attention, "Come on Savannah, let's watch the Little Mermaid again."

"Ok Jamie." Savannah said. "I still want to be home now."

Chris, watching his speedometer fall further and further. Ten miles an hour now. And that's when they were moving. A lot of the time had been just sitting still on the highway as the snow came down harder and thicker. The windshield wipers had been working at their maximum for the past 40 minutes. Forty minutes and Beckley was only ten miles in the rear view mirror. Still 50 miles to go to Charleston and at this rate God only knew when they would make it. The phone rang…

"Hi mom"

"Hey Chris. Wanted to see how you and the kids are making out."

"Not really well, I'm afraid." "We are dead set in the middle of this storm and I'm not sure when we're going to get through it."

"Where are you now?"

"About 10 miles out of Beckley but not really moving. At this rate I'm just hoping they don't close down the interstate and leave us stranded."

"Well the good news Chris, is that if you're able to make it north of Charleston to Pt. Pleasant, just before the Ohio border on Route 35, you should have clear sailing the rest of the way until you get home to Columbus. Looks like home is getting hammered with snow right now and is likely to throughout the rest of today and tonight."

Beckley to Pt. Pleasant is normally a two hour drive, or a little more than 1 Little Mermaid, but today, that will take much longer.

"Ok. Thanks mom. We'll keep you posted on our progress, or lack thereof. Right now, I need to concentrate on the road."

"Be careful. I'll call you if anything new comes up.

"Ok, Thanks. Goodbye."

Chris hung up the phone as he ascended up another incline in the Appalachian mountains. He was one of the lucky ones. As he looked to the side of the road, cars were strewn like garbage cans on garbage day. When he and Linda first returned to Ohio from the Outer Banks, the first decision Chris made was to always have a vehicle with all-wheel drive. Those on the side of the road fishtailed their way to where they now stopped. Not being able to continue any further. Chris continued with a semi in front of him, one behind and one in the lane next to him. At least he thought it was a lane. The snow had been coming down so fast and furious that lanes were no longer evident.

Chris was worried. Even though he had all 4 wheels engaged with the road, he didn't know if he had enough momentum to take him up the next incline. It was steep and they were just inching along. Part of the problem was that others tried but couldn't make it up the hill, so they had to be pushed to the side of the road. Making it even slower for those behind. S...l...o...w...l...y, Chris crept up the incline until finally they reached the summit. It was then that he realized that going up was the easy part, going back down the other side was going to be the hard part. He would have to maintain his lane and speed despite what the law of gravity had to say. Traffic in front of him had opened up now as those that didn't make it up were no longer on the road. Chris eased the car down the mountain. Still leaving the hazard lights on and not daring to bring the car past 4o miles an hour. If the road was straight coming off the mountain, that would have made the descent easier, but it wasn't.

It twisted and it turned. Without being able to see the lanes, this proved to be a most difficult and dangerous undertaking. Chris eased the car along. He could tell that the kids in the back were a bit nervous too as their chatter had almost ceased altogether allowing Chris to maintain his concentration on the task at hand. Chris crept along. Never gaining speed above 40, but not having to lower it to as little as 10 miles per hour either.

According to his calculations when leaving Charlottesville, Chris had expected to make Charleston, West Virginia somewhere between 245 and 3 that afternoon, depending how long they would spend having lunch. Chris glanced at the dashboard clock again, it was now 430. In what should have taken approximately an hour between Beckley and Charleston had taken closer to 2 hours and 45 minutes. But he was not out of the woods yet. He still had to make his way to Pt. Pleasant, which was still about an hour away, in good driving conditions. Just outside of Charleston, Chris decided he needed a break. He would attack the second leg of the storm after he and the kids got out of the car a bit and use the bathroom and grab another coffee. He found a Hardee's at the bottom of an exit ramp and pulled in. Perhaps there may even be some truckers in there that could give him a road report up ahead.

Not thinking when they left Manteo, North Carolina nearly 11 hours ago that they were going to need winter coats and hats, the kids were in the backseat in shorts and t-shirts. Chris grabbed the beach towels and wrapped each child in one and ushered them quickly into the warm building. They then went through their usual bathroom routine; Jamie taking Savannah into the ladies room while Chris stood outside the door. When they finished using the facilities Chris hurriedly got them back to the car that was already starting to cool down. Keeping them wrapped in beach towels, he got them seat-belted in and started the car.

Chris locked it behind him and ran in to use the men's room himself. At the urinal next to him was a trucker who had just come from the direction that Chris and his family was heading. The trucker reported that the first ten miles out of Charleston would be pretty hairy, the rest of the way would be clear sailing.

Back out to the car, Jamie unlocked the door for her dad as he eased himself behind the wheel. He pulled into the drive-thru and got the kids each a hot chocolate and himself a large coffee.

With hot chocolate in hand and a whipped creme mustache on her face, Savannah asked "daddy, how many more Little Mermaids till we're home? I already watched 4 and Eric said we're still in West Virginia."

"I'm not really sure right now pumpkin. The snow is really bad and I need to go slow so we get home safely." "After you finish your hot chocolate, why don't you try to take a nap, maybe when you wake up we'll be close."

"Ok daddy, I'll try."

Chris eased the car back onto the interstate. He took the split to I-64 west. This is where I-77 and I-64 no longer run together. His next exit would be for State Route 35 north to Pt Pleasant and onto Ohio.

Chris activated the bluetooth on his cellphone and called his mother. It was close to 5 now and he was looking to see if he could get a weather report for up ahead.

"Hello?" Said a voice that wasn't his mothers.

"Hi, who's this?" Chris wanted to know.

"Hey Chris, it's Jennifer. Your mother stepped into town for a few minutes. She asked if I would keep an eye on the weather channel with her phone in case you might call."

"Ok. Good."

"Where are you guys Chris?" "I would have expected you to be home by now."

"Yeah, me too, but we just left Charleston, West Virginia. We're still at least 3 hours away." "Anything new on the storm?"

"Nothing new on the weather channel at all, but just before you called, I did look at road conditions on the internet. It looked bad between Beckley and Charleston, but it appears you may have made it through the worst part."

"I hope, for sure. Can you do me a favor?"

"Sure, what do you need?"

"Can you log back onto the computer and look at the road website you were looking at? I need to get off I-64 at Route 35. If the Department of Transportation here in West Virginia is having a hard time keeping I-64 clear, I'm afraid of what I may find on Rt 35.

"Sure. Give me a few minutes. Can I call you back?"

"Thanks. Yeah. That's fine."

"Ok Chris. I'll call you in a bit.

"Thanks."

"Hey Chris?"

"Yeah?"

"Be careful please."

"I will."

With that Chris disconnected the phone and continued his westward, white knuckle driving. Five miles out of Charleston, and as promised, it was still hairy. At least he knew that in a few minutes the snow should significantly slow down and conditions should get better dramatically. Chris peered in the rear view mirror at his kids in the back seat and thought to himself how lucky he was that they were so well behaved and reasonably adjusted despite the tragedies that they've had to endure. They were much too young, he thought, to have to go through losing an aunt and a mother to breast cancer. He never verbalized it, but he feared for his daughters. He knew that if the BRCA-1 cancer gene had so aggressively attacked Linda's family, then there was a reasonable expectation that his girls may one day have to fight the same fight. The doctors say there was only a 50% chance of them inheriting the gene, but that was the same 50% that every other woman in the family had, yet 100% of them ultimately got it. There were no guarantees in life but for now, Chris didn't want to think that far into the future.

Just then, Chris' phone rang, startling him out of that train of thought.

"Hello?"

"Hey Chris. Jennifer. So I went onto that website to check Rt 35. it didn't give me any information. It apparently only gives interstate reports."

"Ok, thanks for trying."

"But," Jennifer continued, "I did call the highway patrol post in Charleston to see what information they might have. They told me that the exit ramp itself is very snowy and icy. They're thinking about closing it down, but probably won't do that for another hour, so you should get through there ok. But when you get off 64, please be sure to take it very slow and very easy. They also told me that the first few miles heading north are very snow covered. You can't see the lanes at all. But, once you get past that and into Winfield, the roads and the weather improve dramatically."

"Well that is certainly good news. Thanks Jennifer."

"You're welcome Chris. I'll keep monitoring for you, should anything new come up I'll give you a ring back. Oh, and Chris?"

"Yeah?"

"It was 70 and sunny today in Manteo. Just something to keep in mind while debating your decision this upcoming week."

"Yeah, thanks for rubbing it in, but I have already thought of that, and trust me, that is a big check mark right now in the pro column of things."

"Ok Chris. We'll be here if you need us. Drive safely."

"Thanks I will."

With that Chris went back to his white-knuckle driving, using every ounce of energy he had focusing on the road ahead. Thankfully after leaving I-77 and moving west onto I-64 the traffic thinned out. Most continuing north. Chris didn't need to worry so much now that he was actually in a lane since he was about the only car on the interstate.

Chris glanced down at his GPS app running on his phone, only another 7 miles until the Rt 35 exit and smooth sailing once he hit Winfield.

"Daddy, I can't sleep!" Savannah said from the back seat.

"That's ok pumpkin. Maybe Jamie can help you find another movie to watch. We should be out of this snow real soon and then we'll be driving faster to get home."

"Can I watch Beauty and the Beast daddy?"

"Sure you can. Jamie can you help your sister please?"

"Ok dad. I'll take care of it" said Jamie.

"Papadopoulos, you ok?" Eric asked.

"Yeah, boy. Thanks. Just really tired and really tired of all this snow. A few more miles and we should be out of the worst of it."

"We should've stayed longer at grandma Pat's."

"Yeah. We probably should have."

Chris, with the snow starting to lighten up, could see their exit up ahead. He lightly applied the brakes in anticipation of slowing down for it as the car went into a sudden skid.

"Whoa!" Chris shouted from behind the wheel as he started to lose control of the vehicle.

"Daddy!" Savannah screamed from the back, and started crying.

The car did a complete 90 degree turn in the middle of the interstate as the back end fishtailed out from behind him. Chris now sat in two lanes sideways, completely exposed to any other traffic that might come over the rise and t-bone them without knowing they were sitting there. Chris put the car in reverse and then rocked it into forward. Even with the all-wheel drive, Chris was having a difficult time getting the car to move. He continued....reverse.....spin the wheels....drive.....spin the wheels....reverse.....spring the wheels....drive.....and so on. Just then a semi came over the rise and had to swerve, narrowly missing the stuck car. Thankfully the trucker was in the far left of the three lane highway. Chris thought for a moment the trucker might stop to help, but then as his tail lights disappeared into the snow ahead, Chris realized that the trucker himself was likely to also get stuck if he stopped his rig in this.

Reverse.....spin the wheels.....drive....spin the wheels....reverse.....spin the wheels.....drive. Finally, Chris noticed some traction as the car crept slowly forward. At least now, they were only blocking one lane. But then became stuck in the snow again. Chris, the three kids all dressed in shorts and t-shirts were stuck on a blizzard covered highway in the West Virginia mountains. With no idea how they were going to escape. Chris got out of the car in the snow, trying to clear whatever snow he could from in front of the car, but with no coat or gloves, he wasn't able to get much accomplished.

Just then, from behind them, Chris saw flashing lights in the sky above the rise in the road. They were yellow lights, like you would find on a tow truck, as opposed to red or blue lights like on a police car. The tow truck came into view from behind and stopped just before hitting Chris's car. The tow truck driver got out of his truck and up to Chris' window.

"My brother called me" the tow operator said to Chris. "He was the rig driver that blasted past you about 15 minutes ago. Saw that you were stuck and knew I was just down the road." "Where you trying to get to?"

Chris, so thankful of his sudden good luck told him, "ultimately back home to Columbus. But right now, just off here and onto Rt 35. I heard that once I hit Winfield up the road a bit I should be good to go weather wise the rest of the way home."

"Well, I'm not sure how the weather is outside of West Virginia, but I do know that it is a sight better just north of here. Luckily I live in Winfield and was just heading home. Let's get you hooked up and I'll take you and your family into the clearing weather so you can continue on."

"Really?!?!?! Thanks! That is so cool of you to do!"

"No worries. Going there anyway. You're not really supposed to ride in a towed car, but I don't have room for all of you in the tow truck. I don't think anyone will bother us in this weather."

A few minutes later and the truck was hauling Chris and his family off the interstate and onto Rt 35. As promised, the exit ramp was very snow covered and slippery. The tow driver took it slow as he maneuvered both truck and car down the ramp and took a right, heading north into Winfield. Almost like someone threw a switch, a couple of miles past the exit ramp the snow had come to a complete stop. There was snow on the ground, but nothing like it had been since Chris and the kids left Beckley. Perhaps their luck was starting to change. A few minutes up the road, and the tow truck driver pulled into his service station.

As the tow truck operator jumped out of the truck to disengage the car from the harness, Chris jumped out of the car to pay him.

"Friend, no payment is needed. I was coming home and heading this way anyway. I'm happy that I was able to be of help to you and your family."

Chris, taken aback by the driver's generosity, simply said the only thing he could, "thank you so much. You don't know how much I appreciate what you've done for me and my family."

"I was happy to friend. That's how we do in the south. Neighbor helping neighbor. Even if the neighbor is a yankee!"

Both men laughed as Chris shook the tow truck driver's hand and got back behind the wheel of his car. He took notice of the name of the service station as he pulled out. Chris would be sure to do something nice for the man who saved both he and his family from the cruel bitch called Mother Nature.

Rt 35 leading north out of the town of Winfield was not exactly clean and dry, but was significantly better than what Chris had been facing the last several hours. At least the snow hadn't accumulated on the street and he could see the actual road.

Chris, glancing down at his GPS, noticed he had he had 154 more miles to go before arriving home on Hibiscus Court in Westerville, a middle class suburb of Columbus. In typical driving conditions, that should easily be done in just about two and a half hours. Today, Chris was just hoping to be able to do it in three and a half. It was now close to 5:30, they've been on the road approximately 12 hours already.

As the weather reports indicated, the roads and the weather did significantly improve as Chris put towns like Buffalo and Southside, West Virginia in his rear view mirror. Finally, in the front windshield of the Jeep Cherokee was the Ohio River and the Buckeye State. Never before had Chris been so excited to see the town of Gallipolis, Ohio.

The rest of the trip up Rt 35 through Ohio to Chillicothe had been the easiest part of the drive since leaving Virginia. Chris was motoring along as Savannah proclaimed that "One Black Beauty was now over."

Chris could do nothing but laugh at his youngest. "Ah, the joys of being so young and innocent. When your biggest concern is how many viewings of your favorite movies it would take to get home," Chris thought to himself.

"That's great pumpkin!" Thanks for keeping track for me. I'll tell you what, I'll bet if you watch it just one more time, we will be real close to home when its over."

"Ok daddy. But I've seen this movie like a million times, but if it will help you drive better, I'll watch it again."

"Thanks princess. I can always count on you to help me."

"You hear that Eric? Daddy says I help him. He never tells you that, 'cause you're bad!"

"Dork"

As Chris got to Chillicothe, he pointed the car further north onto Rt 23. Now into the homestretch when his cell phone rang.

"Hi mom. Yeah, we made it out of the storm. In Chillicothe now. How's it look ahead?"

"You should be fine Chris until you hit I-270. You pick the storm back up at that point."

After a momentary pause, Chris replied, "Really, tired of all this snow. But it's good to know that I will only be in it only a little bit more. I'll call you when we get back home."

I-270 is the outer loop encircling Columbus. Chris will gain access to it on the Southwestern part of Columbus, but will need to make his way to the Northeast side to home in Westerville.

Chris made it to I-270 with no problems, in fact, he made it onto I-270 without incident. For a split second he thought that he perhaps had beaten the storm. That thought went immediately away when he got to Obetz, and the snow maker came back with a vengeance making it almost impossible to see. The snow came straight at the windshield, and with now, almost 14 straight hours behind the steering wheel it seemed to hypnotize Chris as he plowed forward bit by bit. The day had turned into night about two hours ago and the street lights were of no help at this point. The storm completely blotted them out.

That was it. Chris just simply couldn't go any further. Fourteen hours behind the wheel of the Jeep Cherokee, a mere 30 miles from home and the family had to stop for the night. Luckily, Chris knew of a Holiday Inn Express at the foot of the next exit and made his way towards it.

"Papadopoulos, this isn't our exit!" Eric shouted from the back seat.

"Yeah, boy, I know, but I can't go any further. Help me out and wake up Jamie. Ask her to get Savannah wrapped in that beach towel again so we can run into the hotel. We're going to have to stop for the night."

Eric took the opportunity to slug his older sister in the arm. "Hey Jamie, pops wants you to get Savannah wrapped in a towel. We're checking into a hotel for the night."

"Ow!" Jamie yelled out. "Why do you always have to be mean. I think you have rage issues."

"Why do you always have to be a dork?"

"Kids, please just stop! I'm exhausted. Please just get along."

"Sorry dad" both said in unity.

Just then, Savannah noticed that the trip had come to an end at a hotel and yelled out, "daddy can we go swimming? You always take us swimming when we go to a hotel."

"Sure pumpkin. We'll check out the pool."

"What about food papadopoulos? We haven't eaten since lunch?"

"Well boy, there's no restaurant in the hotel, but grandma Pat did pack us some food before leaving that we haven't touched yet. We'll eat that."

"A picnic in the hotel? Yay!" Savannah squealed.

Then, after running from their car to the entrance of the building, a very tired Chris and three young children checked into the Holiday Inn Express - Obetz for some swimming and a picnic dinner.

CHAPTER 12.

Chris threw the suitcases on one of the two double beds in their second floor room. He took the picnic basket that grandma Pat had packed and placed that on the small table. With only two chairs at the table, Jamie and Savannah spread out a large beach towel on the floor and sat there. Inside the picnic basket grandma Pat had packed sandwiches for each. Ham and Cheese on rye with mustard and four apples. She even managed to throw in a large banana bread for good measure.

While the kids started in on their food, Chris ran out to the vending machine down the hall to get 4 Pepsi's to wash it all down. By the time he had gotten back to the room Eric was already done with his sandwich and apple and was digging through the suitcases.

"Boy" Chris said sternly. "What are you rummaging for?"

"It's only a matter of time pops, before Savannah starts whining about using that swimming pool, so I'm looking for our bathing suits."

"Well, just chill out a bit. You just ate, you can't go swimming right away." Chris knew the whole wait an hour after eating to go swimming was an old wives tale, but he needed some down time before taking the kids to the pool. Chris then grabbed the banana bread and broke off pieces for each of the kids. "Besides, I do have to call your grandmother to let her know we're in for the night. I know she'll be worried about us."

"Don't forget to tell grandma that we're at a hotel and that we're going to go swimming daddy," Savannah chimed in, trying to be helpful.

"I will princess. Jamie, when you two are done with your banana bread, can you take your little sister to the bathroom and get her into her bathing suit?"

"Sure dad. Was already planning on that."

"Then you go change next boy."

"10-4 papadopoulos"

While the kids got themselves ready to go swimming, Chris called his mother to report in and then, wearily, took the 3 kids down to the pool.

CHAPTER 13.

It was another fitful night of sleep. You'd think that with 14 hours of time logged behind the steering wheel in a blinding snow storm sleep might have come easily. But each time Chris closed his eyes, all he saw were the white lines of the road and the huge snow flakes hitting the windshield. And every time he tried to take his mind off those visions, the looming decision of whether to relocate the family kept him lying awake.

Finally, as the first rays of daylight creeped in between the crack in the black out curtains of the hotel room, Chris got himself out of bed. He was surprised at how stiff his body was, seemingly from him being tense from Beckley, West Virginia until they got to the hotel last night. Chris quietly made his way to the bathroom. Afterwards, as quietly as he could, Chris struggled to change out of his sweatpants and into a pair of jeans. The sudden activity in the room startled Eric awake.

"Pops, where are you going?"

"I'm going to run down to the lobby and check in with the front desk about the weather and road conditions. Maybe grab a cup of coffee too. You stay here with your sisters, I'll be right back up."

Chris made his way to the elevator. It was about 7am. He knew the day shift of the hotel would be coming in at this time and they could give him a report about the roads.

Chris hit the "L" button in the elevator and made his way from the second floor down to the lobby, feeling a little lazy that he didn't just take the stairs.

As the elevator doors opened, Chris saw the breakfast area set up and ready to go for the hotel guests. He decided to grab a cup of coffee first. Likely he would need a good bit of coffee to get through the day today. He knew that once home he would need to get everyone unpacked, laundry done, make sure the kids had everything they will need to go back to school the next day following their spring break vacation. He will need to make their lunches, get them in baths and off to bed before he can worry about doing anything for himself.

With coffee in hand Chris approached the front desk clerk. According to the name tag, his name was David, but he looked like "the dude" in the movie "The Big Lebowski." "The dude" was not looking at all happy to be there this Sunday morning.

"Hi David, my name is Chris, I'm up in room 204. I just wanted to see how your drive into work this morning was. My kids and I are anxious to get home ourselves."

"Well, I wouldn't know, said David. I've been here all night. The girl who is supposed to relieve me hasn't made it in yet. She called about a half hour ago saying she has already been on the road a half hour but the driving was slow, and she lives less than 5 miles away!"

That did not warm Chris' heart, knowing that he had at least 6 times that distance to cover to make it back home. As cheerfully as he could muster, Chris said, "well, I hope she gets here soon and that you make it safely back home."

David, still with a frown on his face merely said, "I'm not even gonna try it. I'm just going to take a room here and sleep until I have to come back again tonight."

With that Chris refilled his coffee cup and went back to his room. On the way up, he decided that he'd let the kids sleep as late as they wanted. Well, as late as Eric and Savannah wanted. If he let Jamie sleep as late as she wanted, they might as well move into the hotel. This thought broke Chris' bad mood and he felt a smile sneak across his face.

When Chris got back to the room, he found all three kids asleep. Chris decided to just sit in the dark in one of the chairs at the small table that hosted part of their picnic the night before. He sat there sipping on his coffee mulling over in his brain that pro and con list once again for taking, or not taking, John Clark's job offer. Chris would've thought that driving through the snow yesterday would have made the decision that much easier. If they took the offer, it's likely they wouldn't have to endure storms like this very often. But the truth is the closer he got to his home in suburban Columbus, the deeper the resolve became to stay. As Chris endured the bad roads and miserable weather he thought how much he wanted to be in his safe haven. That image was the home he and Linda had created for him and their three kids. Ohio was "home" he thought, the Outer Banks was just a daydream. It wasn't reality. It was a place that people moved to in their early 20's, as Chris and Linda had. Or it was a place you moved to when you retired as grandma Pat did. It wasn't a place you moved a family.

As Chris was settling in on the thought of staying in Ohio, Savannah had woken up.

"Daddy, are we going home today?"

"Yes pumpkin. Just as soon as everyone wakes up, we'll get ready and leave."

"Daddy, you know Jamie won't get up! We'll be here forever!"

"Good point Savannah. As soon as Eric wakes up we'll get ready and leave."

"Want me to wake him daddy?"

"You don't have to dork. I'm already awake since you won't stop talking!"

"Daddy! Eric says I always talk. I don't always talk do I daddy?"

"No princess you don't. You just have important stuff on your mind and you want to let us know about it."

"See Eric" Savannah explained. "Daddy says I just talk about important stuff!"

"He was just being nice. He really meant that you talk ALL THE TIME!"

"Daddy!"

Just then, miracle upon miracle, Jamie was awake!

"Come on, Savannah" said Jamie, while wiping sleep from her eyes, "let's get you in the bathroom to brush your teeth and to get changed so we can get back home."

"Thanks Jamie" Chris said. "Eric, while they're in the bathroom, why don't you get dressed while I check in with your grandmother."

A short while later the girls came out of the bathroom wearing the clothes they wore a week earlier when they left Ohio. Jamie was in jeans and an Ohio State sweatshirt, Savannah in a pair of black pants with a pink Radio Disney hoodie. Eric who was dressed in his sweatpants and his Westerville YMCA "Sharks" swim team hoodie went into the bathroom to brush his teeth. The family then filed down to the lobby to grab the continental breakfast that the hotel provided.

After getting the kids situated with their waffles, cereal and fruit, Chris went back to the front desk to check to see if the morning staff had made it in. David, "the dude" was no longer at the desk, but Mary Anne was. As Chris approached the desk, Mary Anne with a huge smile asked how she can help.

"Hi" Chris said, "the kids and I were forced off the road last night and couldn't make it home due to the snow. I just wanted to ask what the condition of the roads were."

"I live about 5 miles from here" Mary Anne said as she took a loose piece of her blondish hair and tried tucking behind her ear, "and it took me well over an hour, but I take mostly back roads. As I understand it the freeways, while still mostly snow covered are passable."

While not overly excited about the report, Chris thanked Mary Anne and rejoined the kids for breakfast.

"Daddy, can we go back in the pool after we eat?" Asked Savannah

"I'm sorry pumpkin" Chris replied, "but I think its best if we just get on the road for home."

"Ok daddy, but how many Little Mermaids will it take till we get home?"

"See papadopoulos? She's always gotta be talking?"

"Daddy! Eric is being mean again!"

"OK kids, finish up so we can get back home."

It was about 30 minutes later and the family was back in the car and ready to go home. Chris looked at his clock on the dashboard. It showed 10am. To himself he hoped that the 30 minute drive would "only" take an hour or so. Chris shifted the Jeep Cherokee into drive and they were off....

The roads were not great, but they were significantly better than they had been the night before. Plus the snow had stopped falling. The sun was fighting with the clouds, but some of her rays were peeking through. Driving was slow, but at least there weren't many cars on the road. It looked like Columbus picked up a good 10 inches of snow in this storm. Columbus wasn't like Cleveland. While 10 inches would have been nothing more than a minor inconvenience to the city 150 miles to the north, Columbus didn't have as many snow plows and salt trucks. Ten inches was a big deal in the state capital.

It wasn't the hour that Chris had hoped it would be when they finally pulled into their driveway on Hibiscus Court in Westerville. The clock on the dash indicated that it was 11:19 am. But, they made it home safely. And that's all that mattered.

CHAPTER 14.

After a day of flurry, both snow and activity, Chris got the kids up and ready for their first day back at school following their spring break.

It was still a bit dark out when Jamie, Eric and Savannah all came to the breakfast table still in their pajamas. One thing that being a single father had taught Chris, is how to make meals and keep things moving. He had little practice of this while Linda was still alive, but he had gotten quite good at it during the last several months. And if he was honest with himself, he felt quite proud of it.

"Daddy, can I tell everyone at school today that we're moving to the beach?" Savannah asked.

"No princess, we haven't made that decision yet. Although we'll have to this week. We still need to discuss this as a family."

Eric, always the one who liked to move things along yelled out "All those in favor of moving raise your hands!"

Within a split second both Eric and Savannah threw their arms up in the air. The dissenters were Chris and Jamie.

"Dork!" Eric shouted out to his big sister, "why isn't your hand in the air like its supposed to be?"

"Because I don't vote that way. At least not yet. I have to talk to Rachael again."

"Why? Big sister can't make decisions for herself," Eric mocked.

"You wouldn't understand" Jamie spit out in defiance. "You don't ever take the time to think things through. You're….you're…..just a mentally undeveloped little boy!"

"Yeah," Savannah chimed in. "Whatever Jamie said. That's you Eric!"

Feeling like the father should step in now, Chris replied, "ok, ok, enough!" Finish your scrambled eggs and toast and go upstairs and get dressed for school. Dress warmly, it's still cold out."

"Daddy?" Savannah said softly, "can we decide tonight that we're moving?"

"Pumpkin, I can't promise that we ARE moving, and we really won't have time to decide tonight either one way or the other. You have ballet, Eric has swim practice and Jamie has a volleyball game tonight at the Y."
"Hopefully tomorrow we'll have time.

The kids all went upstairs, got dressed into clean clothes that Chris washed, folded and put away yesterday after getting back home.

Jamie and Eric started their classes first so he dropped them off at the junior high and middle school first before taking Savannah to kindergarten. He then made his way to the radio station for his first day back on the job in over a week.

Things were pretty mundane at the station. Chris didn't bring up the offer from John Clark at Ocean 105, and changed the subject quickly whenever anyone asked how his trip to the Outer Banks went. He merely swept them away with a hand and said "It was nice to see my mother and some old friends again" and left it at that.

After getting off the air at 2 that afternoon, Chris did some production work at the station. Things like recording some commercials and promos that needed to be on-air by tomorrow. He then left to go pick up the older two children and then Savannah at kindergarten.

Once in the car, Savannah felt proud of herself when she said that she told her teacher "we went to go see our grandma Pat on the Outer Banks last week but don't worry, we're not thinking about moving there." "See daddy? You told me not to tell anyone that we're moving so I didn't."

"You did very good princess," Chris said to his youngest while trying to hold in a laugh.

Eric followed up with "do you ever stop talking?"

Chris got the three home, settled in and started on homework while he made an early dinner. They all had to be out of the house and at the YMCA in the next hour and a half.

It was close to 8:30pm now and the young family left the Y, activities for the evening now completed, as they started for home.

"Daddy?" Savannah continued, "I told my ballet teacher what I told Mrs. Josephson, my teacher at school. I told her we went to the Outer Banks but not to worry about us moving. I'm good at fooling people, aren't I daddy?"

Eric couldn't pass it up, "That's not fooling people dork, that's lying!"

"Daddy! Tell Eric to stop calling me a liar!"

All Chris had to say was "Eric Walter!" And his son got the idea.

"But you know sweetie, Eric is kind of right. Maybe you shouldn't try to fool people. Maybe we just shouldn't talk about it at all."

"Ok daddy."

Just then Chris pulled the Jeep into the driveway of the house on Hibiscus. "Jamie, take your brother and sister in for me please. All of you brush your teeth and get your pajamas on. I'll be in shortly, I just want to shovel the last of the driveway real quick."

About 20 minutes later the kids were ready for bed and the entire driveway was clear. Chris had only shoveled it partially yesterday after getting back home from the long trip. Back aching a bit, Chris tucked each one in and promised they'd talk more tomorrow at dinner about the upcoming decision.

Chris quietly made his way into his home office. He thought he might make a quick pros and cons list of this moving or not moving scenario. The scenario that feels like it has kept this family hostage for the past several days. It's all we seem to think about, and largely due to his own fault, Chris thought, a subject we avoid talking about. He opened the laptop on his desk when an email chimed in. Chris opened it. It was from Jennifer.....Hi, Storm and I were just thinking about you guys. I know your mother said it was a rough trip and that you made it safely, but we just wanted to wish you luck in your decision this week and hope to see ya'll soon! Have a good one - Jennifer and Storm

Well that was nice Chris thought. Again, the whole southern hospitality thing that you just don't find in this area. Would it be so bad if this family had a bit more of that in our lives?

Chris typed a reply:

Hey thanks! Yes it was a rough trip. A couple of places there that were a bit scary, I have to admit. I just put the kids to bed and was about to do a pros and cons list when your email came in. I promised the kids that we'd finally talk about it tomorrow after school. Still not sure which way we'll go, but we'll let you know once we've made up our minds. Either way, I'm sure we'll see you soon as I'm sure we'll be back in the summer. Hope you and Storm are well!

Chris

Chris closed his laptop. He didn't feel like putting together that list right now. He leaned back in his chair in the dark....zzzzzzzz

The next thing Chris knew, it was 2:12 in the morning, he was still in his office chair. He got up slowly, stretched his stiff back and thought sleepily to himself, maybe some help wouldn't be a bad thing. He slowly walked up the steps to the second floor, walked passed Eric's bedroom. He checked in on him. Sound asleep. Next he checked in on the girls. Also both asleep, but Chris noticed something he never noticed before. Jamie held onto a picture of Linda as she laid there dreaming her dreams. Chris felt a sharp tug on his heart as a tear started to form in the corner of his right eye. He then leaned over and gently kissed his daughter on the forehead as he made his way to his own bedroom and his own bed. Without even changing out of his clothes, Chris was back asleep.

CHAPTER 15.

The first streak of daylight was creeping into Chris's window as he was startled awake from the ringing of his cellphone. He looked at the time. It was 6:25 am. Five minutes before his alarm is set to go off. Sleepily he recognized the number as his mothers and answered the phone.

"Hello?

"Hi Chris. It's mom. Did I wake you?"

"It's ok, the alarm is going to go off in 5 minutes anyway. What's up?"

"Oh nothing. I ran into Jennifer last night as I was on my evening walk. She said you two traded emails."

"Yeah, we did. Nothing big. She just wanted to wish us luck on our decision."

"Have you decided yet Chris?"

"No mom. But I promise you will be the first to know. Even before I tell John."

"Jennifer mentioned that you and the kids were likely to decide today."

"Yeah, that's the plan. I'm hoping at dinner we can all talk and come to a consensus. Right now Eric and Savannah are on board with it. But they're still too young to know about consequences to actions like this. Jamie, I suspect is still on the fence. I have a feeling it has to do with leaving Rachael."

"I thought Rachael gave Jamie the green light on this." Grandma Pat said.

"She did. But I want them to talk face to face. I'm going to tell Rachael's dad Andy that I'll pick up Rachael from school today and have her over for dinner with us. That way Jamie and Rach can really talk.

"Sounds like a good plan. Let me know how it goes."

"I will mom, but I have to go now. I need to jump in the shower and get breakfast started before I can get the kids up."

"Ok. Love you Chris."

"Love you too mom."

Chris set his cellphone back down on the nightstand, just noticing now that he never got undressed from yesterday. He turned on the shower, brushed his teeth and shaved, then got into the shower and stood under the hot water a good while longer than he normally does. Trying to put off the start of the day, he supposed.

CHAPTER 16.

"Ok boy, time to get up. Get yourself dressed and head downstairs, there's breakfast waiting for you." Chris repeated the same set of instructions when he went into the girl's room to wake them up. Chris then went down and finished making the oatmeal and toast for the kids as they filed down, one-by-one.

Jamie, never was a morning person, but the first to speak, "hey dad, we gonna decide today what's going on?"

"Well, we're going to talk about it. Whether we actually make a decision or not is still up in the air. And by the way, I'm going to call Uncle Andy and have Rachael come over for dinner, she should be part of this conversation too."

"Yay!, Rachael is coming over!" Squealed Savannah.

After breakfast the kids went back upstairs to brush their teeth and to get their winter coats and boots on.

"Sure would be nice not to have to wear this stuff anymore papadopoulos," Eric said as he struggled with his hat and gloves as he came down the stairs.

"Yes, it would boy."

Chris took his usual route in the morning. He dropped the two older kids off first and then Savannah. Before going into the radio station this morning, Chris made a side trip over to the cemetery. He didn't know what he'd find there, divine guidance perhaps, but he wasn't sure.

Chris parked the car in front of both Linda and Sue's graves. There were clear footprints in the snow going up the hill to their plots. No doubt Andy had been here either this morning or yesterday. Chris did his best to stay within the existing footprints as he traveled the hill, to keep his feet as dry as possible. He stood before the reddish-brown granite headstone with his wife's likeness etched into the stone. Off to the right of Linda, a similar likeness of Sue was etched into black granite.

Chris stood there for a while. There was always a stillness about this place. It was just very quiet. More quiet and still than any place Chris had ever been. The traffic from the road out front was too far away to be heard. Chris didn't notice it at first, but hot tears started to drip down his face as he stood there. Chris never really talked to Linda while there. He just thought thoughts, figuring from Heaven, Linda would know why he was there and what he had to say.

After a time, Chris looked at his watch and knew he had to get to the radio station to get on the air. He kissed his fingers and laid them on top of the headstone. He turned and walked down the hill very carefully towards his car in the same footprints he used coming up. Chris realized he must have been there longer than he thought.
The car already had cooled down. He started the engine and turned the heat to high as he left the gravesite, never taking his eyes off the headstone in his rear view mirror until it went out of sight. Chris turned right onto Main Street and made his way to work. On the way he called Andy, let him know that he just left the girls and invited Rachael over for dinner.

CHAPTER 17.

"Hey Chris, glad you can make it," said the morning DJ, Kevin Whelan as Chris came crashing through the studio door and 9:59:30.

"Yep, made it with 30 seconds to spare…"

"Well, I loaded up your commercials for your first break and your next three songs are queued up for you too."

"Thanks Whelan, I owe you."

"No worries. Everything ok?" " I noticed you were a bit preoccupied coming back from vacation yesterday and now this. You're never late for your shift."

"Yeah, I'm fine. Trying to get back into the swing of things. Vacation kind of threw us out of our routine. Just trying to find the groove again."

Kevin knew that Chris was having a hard time since Linda died with everything falling upon his shoulders. "Ok dude, well if you need anything, just let me know."

"I will. Thanks Kevin."

The next four hours went by in a huge blur. Before Chris knew it, it was already 2pm and Todd Mitchell was ready to take over the afternoon drive shift. Looking back, Chris didn't remember a thing about his shift. One minute he was starting, and the next it was over. Likely not my best show Chris thought. He next looked at the production box. Chris checked to see if there was any commercials or promos that he needed to "voice" right away. It turns out there is nothing going on the air today or tomorrow, so Chris decided to put it off. Since there was no extra work after finishing his shift, Chris went over to the Kroger's grocery store to pick up supplies for dinner before picking up the kids from school.

Once he and the kids, including Rachael were back home, Chris got them started on their homework while he prepared dinner. He decided on Chicken Marsala with mashed potatoes. Chris opted for the cutlets earlier at the store so he wouldn't have to pound the chicken flat. While he was in the middle of dredging the cutlets in flour, Savannah made her way into the kitchen. It was only a matter of time Chris thought....

"Daddy? Are we going to talk about moving to the Outer Banks while we're eating dinner tonight?"

"Yes pumpkin. We are."

"Ok daddy, I'll make sure Jamie and Eric know for you."

"Thanks Savannah. But can you do one more favor for daddy?"

"Sure! I love doing favors for you daddy!"

"Can you ask Jamie to come in here please?"

"Ok daddy. I'll come in here with her in case you need me too."

"No, but actually, I could use your help with something else. Can you keep your cousin Rachael company while Jamie is here?"

"Ok."

Savannah turned and went upstairs to Jamie's room to let her know that daddy wanted to talk to her. Eric listening from his bedroom chimed in "awwww, you're in trouble....."

"Just stop it Eric!" Jamie replied. "You just always have to be mean!"

"Yeah! Mean!" Savannah added.

Jamie closed up her math book and went downstairs. She had a feeling she knew what her father wanted but nonetheless entered the kitchen with a "hey dad. What's up?"

"Hey Jamie. As you know we're going to have this moving or not moving conversation at dinner tonight. That's why I invited your cousin. I feel like she should be able to voice her opinion too, since indirectly, she will also be affected. In the little informal vote your brother decided to pull the other day, you were not willing to vote yes. Dinner will be ready in about 30 minutes. I want you and Rachael to put your homework away and have a conversation about it. I know when you last talked on the phone she was all for it, but now I want that decision to be face-to-face."

"Ok dad. I pretty much think she will be ok with it. We have talked about it a lot since, but I will make sure. Can I send Savannah down here to help you so Rach and I can talk in peace?"

"Of course."

Jamie went back upstairs. "Hey Jamie, did dad ground you because you were bad?" Eric asked.

"Hmpffff. Eric sometimes I just want to punch you!"

Eric just laughed, pleased with the rise he got out of his big sister.

"Savannah" said Jamie. "Daddy said he needs you to help him in the kitchen to get dinner ready."

"Ok Jamie. See Rachael? I told you my daddy was going to need my help. He always needs my help!"

The two older girl cousins just rolled their eyes at Savannah and closed the bedroom door to have their conversation.

Savannah, now back downstairs with Chris, helped by setting the table for dinner. "I told Rachael that you were going to need my help. I told her you always need my help."

"Yes pumpkin I do. I'm not sure where I'd be without my little Savannah."

With that, the young girl just smiled.

Dinner was finally ready and as Chris was plating it up he sent Savannah upstairs to let everyone know to wash their hands. By the time they made it down, the salad was on the table as were the glasses of milk and the Chicken Marsala.

"Alright kids" Chris said, breathing in heavily and then releasing it again. "I know you've been wanting to have this talk so I guess now is as good a time as any. Let's remember it would have to be unanimous for us to go before we could decide to go. If even just one of us says no, then we stay here in Ohio. Eric let's start with you. Yesterday you had your little poll of everyone and you said you wanted to go. I want to make sure that you've considered everything. It's going to mean a new school, new teammates in both swimming and baseball. It also means new leagues for each that you're not familiar with. Are you going to be ok with all that? Now keep in mind once we make a decision there's no going back.

"I mean papadopoulos, it is pretty scary and pretty exciting at the same time. I did think about that stuff. And I also thought about having the beach down the street and leaning to surf. I talked to my friends at school and they all think its a really good idea so I'm in. I want to make the move."

"Ok. One vote for yes." Chris said, knowing this would be the score at this point in the conversation. "Savannah?"

"What daddy?"

"What do you think about us moving honey?

"Oh, I think we should!"

"Why do you think we should pumpkin?"

"Well, if we don't move and we stay here, then all those poor kids down there will never get to hear Radio Disney."

"What about leaving mommy here and us being there. Are you ok with that?"

A wrinkle came across Savannah's brow. "I was thinking about that, but then I remembered you said that I have a secret power. So if we go, then no one will miss mommy!"

For a split second Chris regretted having said that to his youngest daughter as Eric blurted out "the only secret power you have is that you're annoying!"

"Daddy!"

"Eric Walter!"

"Sorry pops. She just makes it too easy."

"Ok Jamie. I asked you and Rachael to have a conversation about this. Rach, you know that we think of you as a daughter or a sister rather than as a cousin and niece. I wish it could be that you and your dad come too, but his business wouldn't allow that. Have you two talked?"

"Yes dad, we have" said Jamie.

" I know yesterday you weren't sure you wanted to do this because of having to leave Rach. Have you come to some sort of answer?"

Jamie looked over at her cousin Rachael. Chris could see the tears starting to well in her eyes. Jamie then turned back to her dad and said, "I have just one question first. If we go and live on the Outer Banks, is Rachael allowed to spend every summer with us?"

"Of course. I wouldn't have it any other way. As long as Uncle Andy is ok with it, and I know he would be, then Rach can come down and stay with us whenever she wants and can stay for as long as she wants."

"Ok daddy" as tears streamed down her cheeks, "then I vote we move too."

"Three votes yes papadopoulos! You gonna make it four?" Asked Eric.

Chris now feeling his back up against the wall. He still hadn't gotten the sign he wanted from Linda that everything would be alright if they went. He was so unaccustomed to making these kinds of decisions alone and now he never felt so out of control in his life. "I'll tell you what kids" Chris started. "I have your thoughts. Now let me think them over tonight and I'll have my decision in the morning. I need to sleep on this."

"But daddy we all agreed. You said if we all agreed then we could move." Chimed in Savannah.

"Yes pumpkin, but I have to agree too. And I haven't. At least not yet anyway. I still need to make sure this is what is best for the entire family."

"Jamie and Eric, you two please clean up the dinner plates. Get them loaded in the dishwasher. Savannah and I will run Rachael home."

Usually Rachael would just walk home. She lived just on the next street over and would just cut through the backyards, but there was still a lot of snow on the ground. It was cold and well, Chris wanted to talk with Andy.

While Rachael and Savannah got their coats on, Chris hit the remote start on the Jeep Cherokee to start getting it warm. Likely I won't have to use this very often if we do move south Chris thought. He picked up his cellphone and dialed up Andy to let him know they were on their way and to see if he had 5 minutes to talk.

Just a quick couple of minutes later Chris and the girls were inside Andy and Rachael's house. Pictures of Sue still hung throughout the house and displayed on various tables. Andy led Chris into his study.

"Well Andy, I'm sure you're aware by now, I have a job offer back down on the Outer Banks and I'm thinking about taking it."

"Why are you just thinking about it?" Andy wanted to know. "Ever since leaving that place you have always wanted to return. You talk about it constantly."

"Yes, but that's like you know, maybe one day kind of talk. This is real now."

"Ok. So what's the hesitation?"

"A few things. I don't like the idea of uprooting us from you and Rachael. We've always been there for each other. That would all change now."

"Yes, it would, and it would be difficult at first, but life goes on Chris. God knows, if you and I don't know that first hand, who does?"

"Yeah, I know. And then there's…..and don't laugh at this, but there's a feeling of abandoning Linda too."

"Chris come on. You know that's just silly right?'

"Yeah I know."

"Chris, Linda is dead. Sue is dead, but you, me and the kids, we aren't. You know that Linda would want you all to be happy. Don't worry about the gravesite. I will take care of it the same as I do Sue's. I'll make sure the grass is trimmed, the flowers planted and the headstones are cleaned. Now she won't get as many visits from me as she does from you, but you do know that going there doesn't accomplish anything, right?

"Yeah. I know."

"Chris, this is a no-brainer for you. Your mother is there to help. You have friends there and now Rachael and I have a free vacation spot every year." Andy said laughing. "I know you don't need my blessing, but if it is something you're searching for, well then you have it."

"Thanks Andy. Sometimes you're alright" Chris said smiling.

Chris then hugged his brother-in-law, gathered up Savannah and made his way for home for what he knew would be a fitful night of sleep.

CHAPTER 18.

Back home Chris got the kids ready for bed.

"Daddy?" Asked Savannah as she was putting the cap back on the tube of toothpaste, "you are going to tell us tomorrow at breakfast what you decided, aren't you?

"Yeah, you promised pops," added Eric.

"Yes kids. I promise you that when we have breakfast tomorrow, you will know exactly what we're going to do."

With that, Chris kissed each child on the forehead, tucked them in, and wished them each a good night's sleep.

A good night's sleep. Pfft, not something I'm going to see tonight Chris said to himself as he stepped quietly down the steps and into the family room. Chris knowing he needed to put the subject both figuratively and literally to bed decided to turn on the TV for a bit to get his mind on a different track. The Discovery Channel popped up along with a repeat of "Wicked Tuna - OBX." Chris laughed to himself and looked upwards and said quietly out loud "So THIS is your sign to me Linda?"

Chris watched a bit of the show. It was one he had seen before, but it was always nice to see people on TV that he had at least known on a casual level. The show wasn't on the air back when Chris, Linda and Jamie lived on the Outer Banks, but the fisherman on the show were fisherman back then too. They were neighbors and towns people. He at least knew who they were.

At the second commercial break Chris decided to turn off the TV and try to get some sleep. He slowly climbed back upstairs, not wanting to wake any of the kids. Normally before bed Chris would brush his teeth just like his children, but tonight, he just plopped into bed. Chris looked at the clock on the nightstand, it was 10:27pm.

It was now 12:15am. Chris was still up.

Now it's 1:37am. Had he slept a bit? Chris wasn't sure but he sure feels like he hadn't.

2:19am. Still awake. The ever present battle of Ohio vs The Outer Banks, still in his mind. The stable life that he knew, the schools the kids knew, the routines that they had established OR the potential for more help, a better lifestyle, but still the unknown of North Carolina? These are the thoughts as Chris finally.....drifted....off.....to.....ZZZzzzzzzzz.

CHAPTER 19.

6:30 AM! The alarm on Chris's cellphone goes off. It's James Taylor's "Carolina in My Mind" that wakes him this morning as it had for the last several years.

> "In my mind I'm gone to Carolina
> Can't you see the sunshine?
> Can't you just feel the moonshine?
> Ain't it just like a friend of mine
> To hit me from behind?
> Yes, I'm gone to Carolina in my mind."

Immediately Chris's cellphone rings.

"Hi mom"

"Hi Chris. Big day huh? You ready?"

"Uh, yeah, I think so. But how did you know I was giving my answer to the kids at breakfast this morning?"

Grandma Pat answered Chris how she always did when asked this kind of question, "I'm your mother. I know everything!"

"Ok. Which of the kids called you last night?"

"When you went to Andy's last night to drop off Rachael, Jamie called me and told me about the dinner conversation and how you said that you'd give them your answer this morning. She told me that they voted three to nothing to come down."

"Remind me to ground my oldest daughter, will ya ma?"

Grandma Pat laughed, but then turned more serious. "Well Chris, have you made up your mind as to what you and the kids are going to do?"

"I know which way I'm leaning, but I don't have a 100% for sure answer at the moment."

"Well, you're going to need a 100% for sure answer in a few minutes when you wake them up for school. You promised them that you would and you need not drag this out any longer. Just make a decision one way or another. It's not fair to them otherwise."

"You're right ma. Let me get moving this morning and I'll call you back after I drop the kids off at school."

Chris hung up the phone. Just then 2 emails popped up. Chris looked at them already knowing who'd they be from. One from John Clark; and the other from Jennifer.

Chris opened the one from Jennifer first. It was short and sweet. It read:

"Good luck today. Jamie called Storm last night and told us you'd be making a decision this morning."

Hmmm, Chris thought to himself. My oldest was a little busy bee last night it appears.

Now to John's email:

"Yo, bro. Hoping to hear from you today or tomorrow. Not rushing you, but I do need to make contingency

Chris figured he could answer each of the emails later when he was on the air.

Chris went into the bathroom shaved and showered and went down to the kitchen to start breakfast before waking the kids. When he got down there, Chris was quite surprised to see all three of his children all seated around the breakfast table. Jamie had made toast. Eric had poured cereal and milk. Savannah had set the table.

Eric was the first to speak. "Good morning pops. It was a little like Christmas Eve last night. We were too excited to get a lot of sleep so when we heard you in the shower, we figured we would get up and start breakfast for you."

"I set the table daddy!" Savannah said excitedly.

"Thank you pumpkin. That is a great, big help."

Next it was Jamie's turn. "Ok dad. We didn't bug you about moving last night. You said you'd give us an answer this morning."

"No Jamie, you're right. You didn't bug me about it and I appreciate it, but it sounds like maybe you did have some conversations with some other people last night though."

Jamie looking a bit embarrassed looked down at the table and said "yeah, I did call grandma and Storm. I guess you heard about that huh?"

Chris laughing now, "yes, my phone and email went off first thing this morning. Twice!"

"Ok papadopoulos, it's breakfast, let's hear it."

Chris paused for a moment to form his words carefully. "Before I tell you my decision, let me ask you again, one last time. Do you all three want to move to the Outer Banks? It's ok if you changed your mind from last night."

"I do!" Yelled Savannah. "I want to have the other kids down there to have Radio Disney! Plus I still have my secret power so no one forgets mommy!"

Eric with his usual rolling of the eyes at his sister added "I still do."

"Ok. That leaves you Jamie. I know you at first didn't want to go, but then changed your mind after talking to Rachael. If you don't want to again, that's ok."

This time it was Jamie who paused before answering, "yes, I think we should go."

Chris, now realizing he didn't have an easy out since it was unanimous from the three kids. He took a long sip from his coffee and announced his decision, "The score is 4 to nothing. We're moving to the Outer Banks!"

The two youngest kids let out a huge "Yay!" But Chris noticed his oldest was very quiet. Jamie showed no outward signs of emotion. In fact, Chris had noticed increasingly so that Jamie, since the death of her mother, often held in her emotions. Afraid to let them go.

"Jamie. You ok with this?"

Jamie looked down and nodded her head yes.

"You already voted Jamie. You can't change your mind now," added Eric.

"I don't want to change my mind nerd. I'm just mature enough to know that moving is going to be harder than you think it will be."

"You're sure you're ok with this decision?" Chris asked his oldest again.

"Yes, I'm fine. I think we should go."

"Yay!" Shouted Savannah again. I'm telling my teacher today not to give me homework tonight because we're moving!"

"Hold on there just a bit little girl. Yes we are moving, but we're not moving tomorrow. In fact we won't be moving until school is out at the end of May. So that means you still have to do your school work until then."

"Boy you really know how to take the fun out of an exciting announcement, don't you pops? Eric added.

"Alright. Everyone finish up your breakfast and go up and get dressed and ready for school. We have volleyball, swimming and ballet again tonight, but tomorrow we'll start putting together a plan for moving."

"Can I tell my teacher and friends at school today that we're moving to the beach?" Savannah wanted to know.

"Why don't we just wait a day or so first. I need to talk to Mr John today to let him know I'm taking the job. I just want to be completely sure of everything before we start telling people."

"Ok, daddy, but it's going to be hard to hold it in very long" Savannah answered.

"Dork, you can't even keep secret what you had for breakfast. I don't know how you're going to keep this secret."

"I will to Eric!. You wait and see!"

"Ok kids" Chris interrupted. Go upstairs and get ready. I need to make a list of people I need to call today."

CHAPTER 20.

Chris dropped the kids off at school in the same order as always. Jamie and Eric first; then Savannah. He had left the house a few minutes early because there was one other stop he had to make before going into work. When he pulled into the cemetery he was surprised at what he saw.

"What are you doing here? You don't usually make a trip out here, especially this time of day." Chris exclaimed.

"I knew you would be out here after dropping the kids off at school," said Chris' brother-in-law Andy. "I wanted to show you that I would make good on your promise to take care of Linda's grave. But now that you're here, I'll leave you to your thoughts."

Chris watched as Andy made his way down the grassy hill. Being careful with each step as it was still slippery from the morning dew and the recently melted snow. Andy got into his car, tossed Chris a quick wave of the hand, and was off. Chris then turned his attention back to Linda's headstone. Though Chris didn't normally talk out loud while at the cemetery, today he did.

"Well Linda." Chris said quietly, "Today has been the toughest day since you died. The kids and I are moving back down to the beach. I hope you don't think we're abandoning you here, but I think that it really is the best for everyone. The kids will have my mom to help out with homework and a stable home life.

We have new friends down there that we've just met that seem very nice. And you remember John and Uncle Danny. Well, the Uncle is retiring finally and John offered me his air shift. Andy and Rachael are ok with us going and Andy promised to take care of both you and Sue. I hope you're not mad but I do think it's the same decision you would have made. It's times like this that I always ask myself, "what would Linda do." And I do think this is what you would do."

Chris wiping a tear or two from his eye, made his way back down the hill, also being careful not to slip. He got in his Jeep, looked back up at Linda's grave and promised to bring back all the kids before they left for the Outer Banks. Chris then put the Jeep into gear and slowly made his way through the maze of the cemetery and turned right onto the street.

Once on the road, Chris connected the Bluetooth on his phone to the car and placed the first of what seemingly would be several calls today.

"Hi mom."

"Hello Christopher" was the response back. "How did breakfast go?"

"Yeah, breakfast was fine. We made the decision to move."

"That's wonderful son. Tell me how it went."

Chris explained to his mother the events at breakfast. How he called for another vote and Jamie's quietness after the decision was made.

"I'm worried about her mom."

"Yes Chris, it's a tough thing for a teenage daughter losing her mother. She has feelings I'm sure that you can't understand. Just keep her and Eric and Savannah in the Kids Can Cope program until you leave. Let the people there help you with the transition."

"Yeah, that's the plan ma."

"So tell me son," Grandma Pat continued. "How was your visit at the cemetery this morning?"

"How did you know I was there?"

"Christopher I'm your mother. Who knows you better?"

Sheepishly, Chris knew his mother was right. "It was fine ma. Funny thing though, Andy was there when I got there. Seems I might be a bit predictable in my behavior."

"When it comes to Linda, yes you are."

"Ok mom. I'm turning into the radio station now. I've got to go."

"Ok son. We'll talk later about the moving plans."

Chris wasn't really turning into the radio station like he had told his mother. He really wanted some time alone with his thoughts before getting into work. He had to put himself in the right frame of mind before going on the air.

Five minutes later Chris did arrive at work. Fifteen minutes after that, he was on the air. Radio now, wasn't like it was back when Chris first started in the business. Back then he was cuing up 45s and albums. From there, he saw it transition to reel to reel tapes for the music.

And then onto the technology of the future: Compact Discs. Now it had become very sterile. All the music was now on the computer in sound files. All you had to do was load whatever song you were going to play into the software and the computer started each song automatically. As the DJ, you told the computer when to stop playing so you can talk or start the commercials.

While the first song played, Chris was able to pre-load the entire first hour of his shift. That left him time to write a few emails. The first was to John Clark. After writing, erasing and rewriting the email three times, this is what Chris managed to send:

"Bro. I have made my decision (finally). Thanks for your patience in all this. I have decided to take your offer to replace Uncle Danny. I just need to make certain of one thing. I believe you mentioned the Uncle wanted to retire just before Memorial Day. Unfortunately, I can't pull the kids out of school that close to the end of the year. If Danny is ok staying, or if you have some part-timers that can fill in until the first of June, then I'm your guy. Let me know…"

Chris fired off the email to John, then put the computer program in manual so when "Layla" by Derek and the Dominoes finished playing he could give the Central Ohio weather forecast and play his first commercial break of the hour. In doing so, Chris almost slipped and identified the station as Ocean 105. Chris laughed to himself and made a mental note that he had better be careful of this in the future. He wasn't at Ocean 105 just yet.

Once the commercial break was over, Chris announced the "phrase that pays" for today's potential $500 winner coming up later in the show. Today's phrase was "Go Bucks!" A reference to the hometown Ohio State Buckeyes. Columbus was rabid about their Buckeyes.

Once starting the next song, Jay Ferguson's "Thunder Island," Chris put the computer back into auto and turned his attention to his next email.

This one was strange, he thought as writing it. It was to Jennifer. He had only known her for a short time, yet she and her daughter had become central characters into his, Jamie, Eric and Savannah's lives. The email to her was short and sweet:

"Decision made: We're on our way. Details coming…"

With that email sent, Chris thought instantly that perhaps he had jumped the gun. Maybe he should have waited to hear back from John, making sure that the first week of June would work. Boy would he look silly now if all this fell through. It did make Chris resolve to not say anything here at the station until all "t's were crossed and all i's dotted" with John.

With those emails out of the way, Chris went through the rest of his air-shift without once almost saying "Ocean 105." It was one of the most fun shows that he had done in a while. He even had a winner of the "phrase that pays" that day. Jill Nolan of Grove City was now $500 richer, less taxes of course.

Once done for the day with his recording work that needed to be completed, Chris picked up the kids from school so they may start on their busy night of dinner, volleyball, swimming and ballet. Savannah announcing when she got in the car "See Eric? You're stupid. I didn't tell anyone about us moving today!"

CHAPTER 21.

Once back home from the evening's events Chris got the kids ready for bed. Showers, teeth brushed and pajamas on. It was then he was able to open up his email. Besides the usual junk, there were two he expected to see. One from John Clark. The other from Jennifer.

Chris, feeling a little bit nervous about what John may have said, he decided to open Jennifer's email first. It said:

"Hey Ohio! I mean Chris (can't call you Ohio anymore). Storm   and I were so happy to hear the news! We'll plan a big party at   the restaurant once ya'll are down and settled. If there's anything you need in the meantime, just let me know."

She's a funny girl, Chris thought to himself. It will be nice getting settled into a new environment with friends around to help.

Chris went into the kitchen, grabbed himself a Great Lakes Brewing Company Dortmunder Gold. Chris opened the bottle knowing that it would be next to impossible to get his favorite beer in North Carolina. He took a long pull from the bottle, sat back down at his desk and opened John's email:

"Bro! Welcome aboard! No worries on the start date of June. Uncle Danny is scheduled to retire in May but has no plans set in cement yet so he's good on staying till the beginning of June, as long as I give him the long Memorial Day weekend off. I can also fill in with longer air-shifts of the regulars and some part time fill in so don't rush things. Having dinner with Ronnie tonight (yes, she's still around). We'll talk soon."

Chris closed his laptop, emotions swirling all around. Pleased that the logistics have worked out, but still filled with what only can be described as trepidation for leaving his late wife and an overwhelming feeling of what will have to be done in the days ahead. Chris pulled out a legal pad and started his to do list. He needed to write a resignation letter and he will need to hire a mover. Then there's registering the kids at the new schools. And oh yeah, not the least of which put the Columbus house up for sale and find a new place to live on the Outer Banks. Chris, faced with all that needed to be done, wondered if he bit off more than he could chew. Ironically, it was Jamie's words that came back to him from earlier in the day when she reminded her brother Eric that "I'm just mature enough to know that moving is going to be harder than you think it will be." Maybe Jamie is the smartest of all of us Chris said to himself.

Time now to clear his mind. Yes, there was lots to do but he now needed to get some sleep. It was already approaching midnight and he knew his alarm would be sounding at 6:30 in the morning, whether Chris was ready for it or not.

CHAPTER 22.

......And there it was, just as Chris had predicted to himself the night before, 6:30am and James Taylor is singing about Carolina again. Chris stretched for a few minutes and then checked his phone. No new texts or emails overnight. That was good. Chris laid there staring at the ceiling fan as it went round and round, trying to get the motivation to get up and start the day. He knew he didn't have the luxury of taking his time. Not if he wanted to get the kids to their school on time. Finally, Chris rubbed the sleep from his eyes and got up ready to meet the day head-on.

A little while later with all the kids gathered around the breakfast table, Chris announced that it was now official. They can tell their teachers and friends that starting next school year, they will be going to different schools, in a different state. All the while, in the back of his mind, Chris found himself saying "this had all better work out. This whole family is counting on me."

As he often did in these last five or six months, Chris felt overwhelmed, being the sole parent of three small children. He didn't have a wife anymore. Someone that he could bounce decisions off to make sure they were the right ones. He also found himself not doing things that he had done in the past. No more hopping on a motorcycle or taking any unnecessary chances. He was the last parent. Chris often found that to be a pretty sobering thought.

Breakfast finished. Dishes in the dishwasher. Kids in the car. The family of four was on their way to school and work.

"Daddy can I tell my teacher NOW, not to give me homework since we're moving?" Asked Savannah.

"No Princess. I'm afraid you'll never be able to ask your teacher that. We will be here until after school is over."

"Oh darn" Savannah replied. "How about at my new school. Can I tell my teacher that in Ohio we didn't have to do homework?"

"Now princess, you know that would be a lie, and we don't lie in this family. Besides, I don't think they would believe you anyway."

And as if right on cue, Eric grunted out "you're such a dork Savannah."

Luckily at this point Chris had pulled into the school parking lot to drop off the two oldest kids so there would be no further arguments. As Jamie and Eric got out of the car, with lunches in hand, Savannah said "that Eric is so rude."

Sighing heavily, Chris said "that's just how big brothers are. They aren't as nice as girls."

"Were you bad like Eric when you were a boy daddy?"

"No pumpkin. I was the perfect child. Just ask grandma Pat."

"I did daddy. She told me you and Eric are the same."

And now we're moving back to where grandma Pat is, what else will she tell the kids Chris wondered.

Chris dropped Savannah off at school and started mentally formulating the resignation letter he needed to write that day. Fortunately by the time he got to the radio station, he knew exactly what he was going to say.

Chris got into the studio, just as Kevin Whelan was finishing up his morning shift. "Keep an eye on the weather computer" Kevin suggested. "Potential was some severe thunderstorms today. Might even mix with a little thunder snow" he continued.

"Thanks for the heads up Whelan. I'll watch it for sure." Chris continued slowly, "I reckon I'll tell you but please don't mention anything until tomorrow, but I'm going to resign today."

"Moving back to the Outer Banks, huh?"

"Yeah. Wait! How did you know?"

"Well Chris, you ain't been exactly here since you came back from there. You have been so preoccupied. I figured you had something on your mind."

"Yeah. It wasn't like I had been planning this. It was an offer that came up from my old boss when I was down there. And with Linda gone now, well, it's been tough, you know?"

"Chris, I get it. I'd be lying if I didn't say I expected it, but I think it will take the station management by surprise. You know those guys, heads up their, well you know…."

"Yeah. I would just appreciate it if you not mention it right now. I'll be typing up my resignation letter while on the air today."

"No worries, I figure I owe you anyway. You vacated the morning shift to go to middays to be able to take care of your kids. That opened the door for me to do my first morning show."

"Well Whelan, you deserved it. You took mornings and made it your own show. I've been meaning to tell you how proud of you I am."

"Ok. Enough with this mushy mushy stuff. I'm outta here! Good luck with the letter today. I'm sure this place will be buzzing later."

With that, both DJ's bumped fists and Kevin left the studio allowing Chris to get his mind ready for his shift and for writing his resignation letter.

As "Hotel California" came to a close, Chris opened the channel for his microphone and started his show. "Ocean 105, Going back to 1976 for that one, the Eagles with Hotel California. As Whelan told you at the end of his shift, some weather that we'll be keeping an eye on here in Columbus, some possible severe thunderstorms, may possibly even be some thunder snow in the forecast....I'll tell you all about it after this...."

Just as Chris started playing the first commercial, the studio door opened quickly and in walked the station's program director, Chris' boss, Doug Johnson. "Freudian slip there Chris?"

"Oh, hey Doug. What do you mean?"

"Ocean 105? Coming out of the song you said "Ocean 105." You back on the beach, are you?"

"Seriously, I just said that?"

"Yep, play back the tape if you don't believe me, but you did." Doug replied.

Chris looking very sheepishly responded "I'm sorry boss, I guess I have a lot on my mind. Won't happen again."

"Chris, I've been meaning to talk to you. Everything alright? You've seemed so, I don't know if this is the right word or not, but like distant, since coming back from the Outer Banks."

"Well Doug, honestly, I do need to talk to you about something, and I didn't really mean to do it this way, but hold on a second, let me do this…"

(Reading a live tag out of the last commercial)…."And don't forget, big savings going on right now at Hornsby Auto in Westerville. You go down there this week and tell them that Chris Stephens sent you and they'll give you a guaranteed trade in of $2,500 on your used car. But that's this week only at Hornsby Auto in Westerville…."

"I told you a bit ago, possible thunderboomers for our area" Chris continued, "look for heavy rain to hit Franklin County around 11:30 this morning. Some of that rain may mix in with some snow, creating thunder snow. Accumulation is unlikely, but it may be slippery on some of the roads of the city, so be careful out there! Currently its 37 degrees at your official weather station, Capital 102." While saying the last sentence Chris looked Doug Johnson straight in the eye. "Starting off the next three in a row, here's Bob Seger, from 1973 and Turn the Page,".

As the sax from the song kicked in, Chris turned off his mic and turned his direction back to his boss.

"Well, Doug, as I said, I didn't want to do it this way, but I will be handing in my resignation today. My old boss on the Outer Banks offered me the afternoon drive position at my old station."

"Ocean 105, I'm guessing?" Doug asked.

"Yeah. I really had no intention on leaving here, you all have been so good to me and the kids after Linda's passing. Its just become too much for me to handle alone and I do have a support system down there."

"Chris, if I thought I had a chance of talking you out of this I would. But my guess is, you didn't take this decision lightly and have your mind made up."

"I put a tremendous amount of thought into this, trust me. It was stressful too, make no bones about it. It wasn't something I went looking for. It kind of just came to me."

"Well, Chris, you go with my blessing. How much notice are you giving me?" Doug asked.

"The kids still have about six weeks of school left, so we won't be leaving before that. If you want me out of here sooner, I understand."

"Six weeks is good. We've got a few part-timers that I can use to fill in if needed before a full-time replacement is found. Just do me a favor. Don't announce it yet, and jot something down in writing as a resignation for me."

"Will do Doug. I'll get it to you before I leave today."

"Oh, and Chris? One last thing. For the next six weeks can you please remember that we're Capital 102 and not Ocean 105?"

Both Chris and Doug laughed as Doug exited the studio and went back to his office. Likely to begin the search for his new midday person. As promised, before leaving Chris typed up a quick email to Doug:

To: Mr Doug Johnson
From: Chris Stephens
Date: April 16
Re: Resignation

"Please accept this as my formal letter of resignation. My last day of employment will be May 25th, or until you no longer need my services. It has been my distinct pleasure working with you, all the management, and the rest of the radio station staff. I wish nothing but the best for you all."

Short and sweet and to the point, Chris thought. The elaborate resignation letter that Chris had mentally written before work was no longer needed. Before firing the letter off, Chris' finger hovered over the send button for a few moments. All the normal thoughts of "once I send this, there's no turning back" flashed through his mind. And as though directed by a higher power, Chris' finger pressed the send button and the lives of he and his three children had been changed.

The die has been cast. Chris, Jamie, Eric and Savannah were now future residents of the Outer Banks of North Carolina.

CHAPTER 23.

Time over the next few weeks had flown by. So much to get ready before the family's move next week. The family's Columbus house had some touch ups that Chris took care of before putting it up for sale. Chris repainted the family room and refinished the wood floors. He bought new appliances for the kitchen. He also had some flowers planted, trees and bushes trimmed, and a fresh load of mulch spread over all the flower beds. Luckily he did, because three days after all the work was completed, Chris got an offer for the house at full asking price.

As far as living arrangements on the Outer Banks, grandma Pat, John and Jennifer all kept their ears to the ground for a place for the family to live. Chris decided that it would be best to rent for a year, to allow him more time to decide on a place to buy. It was Jennifer that found the yellow, three bedroom, three bathroom house on Croatan Avenue in Manteo, just on the outskirts of downtown, that the family could rent. Going by only his mother's and Jennifer's advice, Chris signed a one year lease on the house located just around the corner from his mother and new friend. It was only through pictures did Chris notice that the house was built in 1908 and was completely renovated and had a wrap around front porch.

So the living arrangements have been solved. One house sold. One house rented. Time to finish packing. The movers would be along in four days to take the family's belongings to North Carolina and there was still so much to take care of. Chris especially, had a tough time with all of Linda's belongings.

Should he take them with him? All of her clothes still remained in the master bedroom's walk-in closest. Even though she had been gone for a while now, Chris couldn't bring himself to remove those things. He still was using the armoire in the corner of the bedroom for all his clothes. Tight space though it might have been. In the end, Chris decided to pack up Linda's things and move them with the family. Perhaps he could donate it to a women's shelter there. He didn't know. But what he did know was that it was less painful a transition for him if he knew that he was bringing Linda with them to the Outer Banks.

The kids did their best to get all of their belongings packed. But kids being kids, there was no rhyme or reason to what they did. One box would be seemingly 100 pounds, weighted down with books. The next box would be as light as a feather with only one stuffed animal in it. He knew that he would have to fix their packing before the movers got here.

That Saturday after dinner, three days before the movers would arrive, Chris had a quick family meeting.

"Kids" he began. "The movers will be here to collect our stuff on Tuesday. Please go through all your stuff again. This will be a good time to set some things off to the side. Things that maybe you don't use anymore, or quite as often. We can donate those things to some kids in the area that might need them."

"You got it papadopoulos" Eric replied.

"But daddy, I never lived in North Carolina before. I don't know what I will need there." Savannah said in a soft voice. "Jamie, you lived there before, can you help me?"

With her chest pumped out, feeling proud, Jamie assured her younger sister, "sure Savannah, no worries."

Of course Eric, never one to miss an opportunity to pick on his sisters, said his usual "dorks."

"Daddy, when are we leaving for North Carolina?" Savannah wanted to know.

"Well, pumpkin, the movers are here on Tuesday since Monday is the holiday. We will help them load up their truck and we will be leaving the next day."

"Does that mean that our stuff will get there before us?" Asked Eric.

"No. The truck will be making a stop or two along the way before delivering our stuff. We'll actually get there a day or two before them. We'll stay with grandma Pat for those days until our stuff arrives. So make sure you pack three days worth of clothes just to play it safe. If the truck takes longer, we can just wash clothes at grandma Pat's."

A few minutes later, Chris ended the family meeting and started getting the kids ready for bed. "Big couple of days ahead of us guys," he said. "We need to get some sleep so we're ready by Tuesday."

CHAPTER 24.

The next few days flew by, like the pages of a calendar on a cartoon to show the quick passage of time. The movers had come and gone and as they were getting ready for the trip to the Outer Banks, their new home, Chris, as a lark, bought a couple of lottery ticket scratch offs at the local Shell gas station as he was filling up the family's gas tank. Much to his surprise, he had won $5,000! "I know just what to do with this," he said to himself as he tucked the winning ticket into his pocket.

Back home, to the now empty house on Hibiscus Court in Westerville, Chris loaded up the kids into the Jeep Cherokee to begin their trip to their new life. Even though it was definitely in the wrong direction, Chris pointed the car towards the cemetery. He had to bring the kids and visit Linda one more time before moving on. He hadn't told the kids of his plan to stop, but they figured it out pretty quickly.

"Going to see mom, before we leave pops?" Eric was the first to bring up.

"Yes boy. We can't leave town without saying goodbye to your mother."

"I was hoping we would." Added Jamie, the one who never wanted to pay a visit to the cemetery. "Seems like the right thing for us to do," she added.

"Daddy? Do I still have my special power?" Asked Savannah.

"Yes pumpkin. You always will. That will never go away. In fact, I'll bet that if one day you have a daughter, she too will have that special power."

"I hope so daddy."

As Chris pulled the Jeep into the cemetery, and following the drive around all its twists and turns to the back where Linda and her sister Sue were laid to rest. Chris was not surprised at all by what he found. Up on the hillside were both Andy and Rachael. The family of four climbed the hill and met up with the family of two. "Andy, I kind of thought I might see you here."

"Yeah Chris," Andy said. I told you that I would look after things here and I wanted you to know that I meant it."

"You really don't know what this means to me. Thank you." Chris said softly, as he fought back the tears.

Rachael had a picnic basket with her and proclaimed that she and her dad thought it would be nice to have a picnic breakfast with their "moms" before the Stephens' moved away.

"Daddy?" Savannah asked. "Does this mean we can't stop at McDonalds now? I wanted an egg Mcmuffin."

"Don't worry squirt," added Rachael. You didn't really think my dad and I were going to cook breakfast did you? We stopped at McDonalds already and got everyone egg Mcmuffins. We just put it into the picnic basket to make it look fancier."

The combined family of six, sat down with their "mothers" under the tree shading the two sisters' graves, and enjoyed their last breakfast together for a while. After eating, each person stood facing both headstones and said their own private goodbyes.

Then with tears in their eyes, they all made their way back down the hill and to their cars. They said their goodbyes to each other. Andy and Rachael will be down to visit over the Fourth of July holiday, with Rachael staying behind until the start of the school year.

Chris turned right out of the cemetery and made his way towards Route 23, then onto Interstate 71 South as the family put the skyline of Columbus in their rear view mirror for the last time. It was now 10:00am on a Wednesday following the holiday. Chris would normally be on the air right now, but Columbus was greeted with a new midday DJ at Capital 102, the young former part-time weekend jock, Bill Halsey, who called himself "The Admiral" was on the air. Chris smiled but felt a bit hurt that he could be replaced so quickly as "The Admiral" started "Wasted Time" by the Eagles...

"You never thought you'd be alone this far down the line
And I know what's been on your mind.
You're afraid it's all been wasted time."

CHAPTER 25.

Chris hummed and tapped along with the radio as he drove the family south and east, and from the rear seat he heard his youngest daughter.

"Just think daddy, I'm going to have lots of new friends because I'm the one who had the idea about Radio Disney."

"Pops already said they're not doing Radio Disney Dork," was Eric's answer.

"Daddy! Eric is calling me a dork again and all I said was that the kids will love me 'cause of Radio Disney."

"Ok kids. It's gonna be a long enough drive as it is. Don't start misbehaving now. And besides pumpkin, I did tell you that it's not my decision to turn the radio station into Radio Disney. I'm only going to work there. I'm not the boss."

"Who's the boss daddy?"

"That would be Mr John."

"Oh, ok. Mr John likes me. I think he'll like my idea when I tell him."

"Dork…."

"Ok kids…."

Jamie, being the big sister, figured she'd help out by keeping the peace, "Come on Savannah, let's watch "The Little Mermaid.""

"How many "Little Mermaids" till we're there daddy?"

"I didn't do the math princess. About 8?"

With that the two girls had their headphones on and watched "The Little Mermaid" for the first time on the return trip to the Outer Banks.

"A little bit better driving weather than the last time, huh pops?"

"Yeah boy, you got that right." With that, Eric settled in with his video game, riding shotgun in the passenger seat.

Chris connected his Bluetooth to the Jeep and turned on Ocean 105 on the Tune In App on his phone. After 2 and half hours, Chris had covered about 150 miles to Winfield, West Virginia. Here he pulled into a parking lot of a service station. As he did, Eric took notice and remarked "hey pops, this is the place where the tow truck let us out, isn't it.?"

"Yeah boy it is. I just have to run in real quick. You and your sisters stay here. I'll be right back."

Chris got out of his Jeep and made his way to the front door, happy to see the tow truck that brought them in almost two months ago, parked to the right side of the building. Chris opened the door as an overhead bell sounded to let the service station staff know that someone had just entered. From out of the back came the scruffy, "Cat" baseball hat wearing guy that hooked his tow truck to the family Jeep.
Chris didn't see his name patch on his green uniform two months ago since he was wearing his work coat, but today Chris noticed his name as "Earl."

"Earl. Hi! Do you remember me?" Chris asked.

"You do look kindly familiar to me." Earl replied.

"It was a couple of months ago. My three kids and I were stranded out on the highway in that freak snow storm and you saved us and brought us here. My name is Chris. Chris Stephens."

"Sure friend. I remember you now. I hope you and your younguns made it back ok."

"We did eventually, thanks in large part to you."

"Well, what can I do for you? What brings you back Winfield way?"

"Well, Earl, when you brought us in, you wouldn't take any pay from me."

"Didn't figure there was a need to. You were stuck. I was driving by on my way here anyway. It didn't put me out none."

"But still Earl," Chris continued. "You did a huge favor for me and my family and as I left here that day, I promised myself that I would remember this place and figure out a way to repay you. I never did figure out how until this very morning."

"This morning? You drove all the way to here for that today? Really friend, there isn't any need."

"Earl, its just a coincidence I guess that I figured this out today. See, the kids and I, we've left Columbus and are on our way to the Outer Banks of North Carolina to our new home. We're relocating there. And when I was filling up the gas tank this morning, I decided to play a couple of instant lottery games. Something I never do. Well, long story short, one of them was a winner and I knew instantly what I wanted to do with the money."

"That's really neighborly of you Chris, but there's no need...."

"You're taking it Earl, please, it would mean a lot to me." Chris said as he put the winning lottery ticket into Earl's shirt pocket, right under his name patch.

Thinking the lottery ticket was probably like $50.00, enough to cover a normal tow, Earl reluctantly left the ticket in his pocket as the two men shook hands. Chris walked back out to the Jeep, got into the driver's seat and headed the car south on Route 35 out of Winfield towards Interstate 64. Earl had followed him outside, waved goodbye to the family as they drove out of sight. As they disappeared over the rise in the road, Earl reached into his shirt pocket pulled out the lottery ticket and screamed out a very loud, WAHOO!

CHAPTER 26.

The ride south went along very easily. A couple of stops for food and gas and they were making great time. Chris figured they would be arriving at grandma Pat's sometime just after 8:30 tonight. Chris switched off the radio on his Bluetooth and hit the contact list on his phone. Figured now would be a good time to check in with his mother to let her know of their expected arrival time. On the third ring, she picked up. Or at least Chris thought it was her....

"Hello, Chris?"

"Yeah, I'm sorry, who's this?" Chris asked.

"Hey, it's Jennifer. Your mother is down at the pool out back getting things ready for you and the kids. She's gonna throw hotdogs and hamburgers on the grill when you get in."

Laughing Chris responded "No, she's not!"

"She's not?" Jennifer asked.

"Well, Jennifer, apparently you haven't noticed the dynamic between my mother and me. Yes, I agree she's probably getting the pool area ready for us. But despite driving ten hours, its going to be me that's going to throw the hotdogs and hamburgers on the grill."

"Well, not sure about all that Chris, but we're all looking forward to you getting here. Storm is really excited to see the kids."

"They're excited to see her too."

From the back of the car Savannah shouted out, " Seven Little Mermaids Daddy! Only one more to go!"

"Thanks pumpkin."

"What was that?" Jennifer asked, being confused by Chris talking to his youngest daughter.

"Oh, sorry, nothing. Just Savannah telling me that we only have one more Little Mermaid to go before we get there."

Again, from the back seat, "Daddy, who are you talking to? Is that grandma?"

"Hold on a second Jennifer" Chris said into the phone. He then turned his attention to his daughter in the back, "no Savannah, it's Miss Jennifer. She and Storm are at grandma's house waiting for us to get there."

"Yay Daddy! Tell Miss Jennifer that we'll be there in just one more Little Mermaid."

"I just did pumpkin."

"And daddy? Can you tell Storm not to leave until I get there?"

"Don't worry princess. She won't."

"Thanks Daddy. I love Storm!"

From the front passenger seat Eric piped in sarcastically, "why don't you *marry* her then?" With the emphasis on the word marry. "Dork!"

"Daddy! Tell Eric to stop!"

Now it was Jamie's turn to weigh in, "yeah Eric, you have rage issues."

"And you two have dork issues" said Eric seemingly proud of his reply.

Chris turned his attention back to the phone. "Jen, sorry about that, I think we're all a bit tired of being cooped up in this car. The kids are getting a little restless. We're close, we only have one Little Mermaid to go......I mean, about an hour and a half left. We're in Chesapeake now."

"No worries Chris. You guys be safe."

"Hey Jen. Would you mind very much doing me a favor?"

"Not at all, what's up?"

"Can you check to see if my mother has a growler of the Lost Colony Blonde Ale? If she doesn't, would you mind running to the brewery down the street and grab me one? I'd sure like to relax with one tonight. I'll give you the money when I get there."

"Sure Chris, but if she doesn't, I have one at home. I'll just run and grab mine instead."

"Thanks Jen. I haven't even moved in yet and already you're helping me out."

"Well, you are a neighbor now, and that's how we do it on the Outer Banks. Be safe. See you soon."

"Thanks Jennifer." As Chris disconnected the phone, a warm glow filled him up. Yes, he thought to himself, that is how "we" do it on the Outer Banks. Suddenly Chris knew he made the right decision.

CHAPTER 27.

It was 8:25 when Chris pulled the Jeep into grandma Pat's gravel driveway. Almost ten and a half hours after leaving the cemetery. Not bad time, he thought. Grandma Pat, Jennifer and Storm all came running down the steps to the driveway to meet the tired travelers. As soon as Chris got out of the car he noticed it.

"Trying to get rid of the weeds in the driveway again, huh ma?"

"Guilty" grandma Pat answered. "You know how much I hate to see weeds in the driveway."

Grandma Pat had a yearly late spring practice of throwing salt down on her her gravel drive and then spraying it with vinegar. She claims it keeps the weeds away. What it does do though, Chris thought, was to give her the only driveway on the Outer Banks that smells like a salad bar. You can smell that vinegar all the way down the street.

Using the elevator on the north side of grandma Pat's house, Chris and Eric started hauling suitcases up to the main level. Since grandma Pat's house was built on stilts, to protect it from any storm surge that the town may incur, the elevator was helpful in getting things in like suitcases and groceries. The problem for Chris was, it only went to the main floor. Chris would then have to lug them off the elevator and up to the second floor where he and the kids would stay until the movers showed up in a couple of days.

A few minutes later, as Chris finished stowing the bags into both the kids rooms and his, Jennifer came up with a cold glass of the Lost Colony Blonde Ale, just poured from the growler. They stepped out onto the back deck overlooking the pool. The kids were down below at the picnic table with grandma Pat cutting and eating watermelon, waiting patiently for Chris to come down and throw on the hotdogs and hamburgers. Just as he predicted.

"Turns out your mother figured you'd want a growler. I didn't have to go home and get mine."

"That's good. Thanks." Chris said. "I just need a minute to unwind before going down to take care of the grill."

"Let me do that Chris." Jennifer offered. "You just drove all day."

"Oh no. No. No. No. No," Chris replied. "You do that and my mother will be all over me. No. It's just easier for me to do it."

"You know best I guess."

They stood out on the deck for a minute when Chris said "that's it isn't?" Pointing to the yellow house who's backyard was backed up against grandma Pat's neighbor to the right. "That's the house we'll be living in, isn't it?"

"Yep, that's the one Chris. As soon as I heard that it was going to be a yearly rental I jumped on it for you before anyone else had a chance to snag it. It's really a nice house for you guys. Completely redone. I think you're going to love it."

"I'm sure we will. Thank you for that, in case I hadn't already thanked you."

"You did, but you're welcome again anyway."

As if on cue, grandma Pat yelled up to her son on the deck, "Christopher, its time to stop lallygagging and time for you to get down here and feed these hungry kids of yours."

"Whatever happened to that deal where you were going to have dinner ready for us every night when I got off work?" Chris asked while laughing.

"Just you never mind" grandma Pat said. "You haven't started work just yet. Now get down here and start the grill!"

"Yes ma'am."

Chris poured himself another Lost Colony Blonde and went downstairs and made the dinner. Along with the hamburgers and hotdogs, grandma Pat had corn on the cob and had made potato salad. While eating, Jennifer announced that she, Storm and grandma Pat will be throwing a little "welcome home" party tomorrow night at Arnold's. John Clark will be there, Annie and her husband Greg (Chris' old partner and the person in the picture with Chris at the radio station) will be there, as will the Bennetts and a guest appearance by Uncle Danny.

It was getting past 10 pm now. The kids, exhausted from their long day, were falling asleep one by one by the pool. Chris carried each one up to their bed and put them to sleep in their clothes. No point in waking them just to have them change into pajamas, he thought. As Chris tucked in the last child, Jennifer and Storm said their good-byes to grandma Pat and Chris and walked back home to their house just three doors down.

Chris helped his mother clean up outside. Grandma Pat, also tired from the day, said to just wait until tomorrow to do the dishes. She leaned over to Chris, gave him a kiss on the cheek and whispered "welcome home son."

CHAPTER 28.

Chris had forgotten that it gets lighter here sooner than it did back in Ohio. Made sense, they were on the furthest point East in the United States.

It was just 6am when the sun came streaming into Chris' bedroom window. The birds had already started their morning songs. It was a beautiful day. Chris stepped out onto the back deck, through the trees he was able to see the sunrise reflect off the waters of Roanoke Sound. Figuring the kids would remain asleep for a little bit, Chris headed downstairs to make some coffee and take a shower. The one thing Chris loved about being on the Outer Banks was being able to take his showers outside in the outdoor shower.

When Chris got downstairs, he found his mother already sitting in the living room with her coffee.

"Morning son. Coffee is ready. Just help yourself."

"Thanks ma."

"Plans today?"

"Yeah. I guess. The mover texted me last night. Said they were hung up a bit on their stop in the Washington DC area, but that they would be in tomorrow at some point. So I thought I would take today and get the kids enrolled in school."

"You want me to watch them for you while you're doing that?"

"No thanks ma. I thought I'd take them with me so they could check out where they'll be spending next Fall. The tough part will be that all three kids will be in three different schools. Jamie starts high school this year. Eric is still in middle school and Savannah in the elementary school."

"Yes son, but thankfully where I am and where you'll be living this first year, they're all within walking distance." The benefits of living in a small town."

Manteo, North Carolina is in fact a small town. Chris always described Manteo as "Mayberry-on-the-Water." While living, local resident Andy Griffith must have thought so too considering he lived here for many years. In fact, he is buried on his property just up the road, about a mile and a half away. Chris looked forward to the small town living. He was especially excited for Dare Day coming up. It's a celebration for the locals of the county on the first Saturday of every June. All of the celebration will just be a short one block walk out of his front door.

Chris drained the coffee in his cup, stood up, stretched, and went to the elevator to go to the ground floor for his outdoor morning shower. As he made his way toward the elevator he swore he heard his mother call him "lazy."

This was one of Chris' favorite things about living on the Outer Banks. The ability to breathe in the fresh air while standing beneath a hot shower. There would be no kids banging on the door to hurry up. It's just him and the singing birds in Mother Nature. Once finished, Chris toweled himself dry, put back on the shorts and t-shirt he wore to come outside and went back up to the main floor, this time using the stairs for fear of being called lazy again.

When Chris got upstairs, he was surprised to find all three kids around the dining room table with grandma Pat in the kitchen making scrambled eggs, turkey sausage and rye toast.

"Grab another cup of coffee and sit down son. Breakfast will be ready in a few minutes."

"Daddy? Will grandma Pat always be making us breakfast?" Asked Savannah.

"No pumpkin. She's just making it for us while we're living here. We'll be moving into our house tomorrow and I'll be making it again."

"Bummer Daddy!" Savannah continued. "Grandma Pat is making us a good breakfast. You just give us cereal a lot."

"I know Savannah, I'll try to be better from now on."

Eric, after downing his big glass of orange juice, contributed to the conversation. "So papadopoulos, what are we doing today?"

"Well boy, the movers won't be here till tomorrow so we're all going to get you registered for next school year."

"Daddy?"

"Yes Savannah?" Chris knew it would be the youngest that would be asking all the questions.

"Daddy, what school am I going to go to?"

"Well, princess, you'll be going to Manteo Elementary."

"Daddy?"

Chris, knowing there would also be a follow up question, "yes Savannah?"

"What school will Jamie and Eric be going to?'

"They won't be at the same school this year. All of you will be at your own school. Jamie will be at Manteo High School and Eric will be at Manteo Middle School."

"Hey pops…"

"Yeah boy?"

"Back in Ohio at school, I was a Mustang. What will I be here?"

"I believe the middle school are the Braves."

Grandma Pat was now bringing over a huge platter of the eggs, sausage and toast and started dishing it out to everyone while adding, "yes Eric, you will be a Brave. Jamie will be a Redskin."

"Sweet, I'm a Brave." Eric said.

Savannah, never one to pass up an opportunity to talk chimed in with, "you're not a brave, you're a dork! Get it Eric? You always call me one and now I called you one!" Savannah laughed so hard at her own joke, she nearly fell off her chair.

Jamie, who had been quiet up to now, which is her nature added, "don't forget, we also have the party that Miss Jennifer and Storm are throwing down at Arnold's tonight."

"Yep. I haven't forgotten." Chris added.

The family plus now too, grandma Pat, finished up their breakfast. Once done, grandma Pat instructed Jamie and Eric to do the dishes. They did not seem at all pleased by that. Chris told Savannah to go upstairs, brush her teeth and get ready to leave. He told the two older kids the same once they finished cleaning. Chris refilled his coffee and then grabbed his phone and went outside to the front porch. The porch, being on the west side of the house, was protected from the morning sun, but it was in the direct path of the setting sun, which was probably worse. Thank God for the ceiling fans, he thought. Chris opened his contact list and dialed up John Clark.

Not surprisingly, John answered on the first ring with "Bro!"

"Hey John, just wanted to let you know we made it. The movers will be here tomorrow. I was thinking that I'd be able to start my shift on Monday if that works for you."

"Should be fine, but bro, let me ask you. Will you be around on Saturday for Dare Day?"

"Yeah, I was planning on taking the kids out there why?"

"Uncle Danny is broadcasting live from there, as he does every year. I thought to announce this transition, we'd have you join him for a bit on-air. Make the announcement with all the locals around. Could you swing that?"

"Yeah, sounds like a good plan. Even if my mother isn't around to keep an eye on the kids, Jamie can watch over them while I'm with Uncle Danny."

"Timing on this bro, couldn't have been better. Uncle Danny retires at the biggest party of the year, and we announce the return of Chris Stephens to the Outer Banks airwaves."

"Cool. Glad it all worked out the way it did then. So I hear you'll be at the party at Arnold's tonight?"

"Yeah, bro. I'll be there."

"Bringing Ronnie with you?"

"Who bro?"

"Ronnie! The girl you were with when I was here a couple of months ago. The one you told me might be the one…."

"Oh! Her. No bro, that was two months ago. We're not still seeing each other."

"Why am I not surprised…."

"Nope. Coming alone tonight. I'm done with women. Might go be a monk or something."

"Uh-huh. I've heard that before. How come you haven't hooked up with Jennifer?"

"Bro, we went out a couple of times. Just didn't match up too well. Always busy with the restaurant. Plus she has a kid. Didn't want to be involved with all that. But you should bro. You two seem to have built a pretty quick friendship."

"Whoa John. Put the brakes on right there! Linda hasn't even been dead a year yet. Waaaay too soon for me to consider anything like that."

"Ok bro. I get it. But something to consider when the time is right."

Chris, wanting to change the subject quickly added, "so what time do you want me at Dare Day on Saturday?

"How about noon? Maybe sit in with Uncle Danny for an hour. Just don't announce to anyone down here that you're taking over for the Uncle between now and then. We want to make it a big surprise on Saturday."

"Ok. No worries John. See you tonight at Arnold's"

"See you bro."

Chris hit disconnect on his phone and sat on the porch enjoying the morning breeze coming off the sound, and songs of the birds while finishing his third cup of coffee of the morning. He closed his eyes and just sat. The birds sounded happier here. Not as stressed or as angry as the birds in Ohio. He knew that was silly, of course. Maybe it was he that was all-of-a-sudden happier and not as stressed. Chris took it all in for all of a minute before his youngest came crashing through the screen door.

"Daddy! I'm all ready to go see my new school. And look! I'm wearing my Outer Banks Princess shirt that we got when we were here last time!"

"That's great pumpkin. You look very beautiful in it. Just like your mother."

"That's because I have a special power, huh daddy?"

"Yes Savannah, you surely do."

Just then it was Eric who made his way out on the front porch. "Ready to go pops."

"Cool boy. Where's your older sister?"

She's upstairs getting ready. I think she's talking to Rachael on the phone too."

"I'll go upstairs and tell her to hang up daddy. So we can go."

"No, that's alright pumpkin. We're in no hurry. Let her talk to Rach."

"But I want to go see my school daddy!"

"You will soon enough Savannah. This move has been tougher on Jamie than it has on both you and Eric. Let her have her space."

Jamie never said that, of course, but Chris could tell. She was particularly vulnerable; a teenage girl without her mother. At a time that she likely needed her most. Chris certainly tried to be both parents to not only Jamie, but to all three of the kids. But deep down, he knew he wasn't doing it very well. He consoled himself with the fact that he was doing his best which included this move to the Outer Banks. More people around to help him and for the kids to turn to also.

Five minutes later, Jamie made it outside to the front porch and announced she was now ready to see the high school. Chris wasn't very familiar with the elementary or the middle schools, but the high school he did know since once upon a time, he was the voice of the Manteo High School Football Redskins on Ocean 105.

CHAPTER 29.

The Stephens family spent the better part of the morning and part of the early afternoon visiting and registering at the three schools. All three kids seemed to be happy with where they will be spending their days starting in the Fall. Chris was happy that each school seemed modern and updated. The administration also seemed very engaged.

Having not had lunch yet, Chris called his mom and told her to meet them at Stripers. Lunch was on him.

Chris arrived before grandma Pat and grabbed them a table on the deck overlooking the sound.

"Jamie?" Savannah asked, "did you ever eat here before when you lived here?"

As if right on cue, Eric responded with "how would she know? She was two when mom and pops moved to Ohio."

Chris intervened with "no pumpkin. Jamie and mom and I never ate here when we lived here. This place wasn't built yet."

"Hey pops, you hear that?" Eric asked.

"What's that boy?"

"Isn't that your new station that they're playing on the speakers?"

With that the table of three middle-aged ladies that appeared to be locals, stopped their conversation mid-sentence and turned their attention to the family in anticipation of some sort of answer.

Whispering as softly as he could, Chris said to Eric "I think it is boy, but it's still a surprise so let's not talk about it."

The three middle-aged ladies appeared to be annoyed in not being able to hear the answer, went back to their lunches.

Just then, grandma Pat made her way to the deck and the family's table, stopping along the way to talk to the three middle-aged ladies. When grandma Pat glanced and gestured over at Chris while talking to the ladies, he had hoped she hadn't spilled the beans about his new job.

"Friends of yours?" Chris asked as grandma Pat settled into her chair at the table.

"Yes, likely will be of yours too, in the not so distant future. They're your neighbors from over on Croatan Ave. One lives next door, the other two across the street. Their families have been here for generations."

"I hope when you looked over at me and gestured that you didn't tell them about me starting at the radio station. It's going to be a surprise announcement at Dare Day."

"Get over yourself son, you're not that big a deal. I just told them that you and the kids have moved into the yellow house on the corner. Signed a year lease on it."

Seeing grandma Pat at our table, Sandy, the waitress came over with an unsweetened iced tea for her. The only person on the Outer Banks, Sandy said, that takes her iced tea unsweetened. "Some sort of a sin in these parts" she said laughing.

After grandma Pat made the introductions and informed her that we have just moved down from Ohio, Sandy said, "Oh, I heard about you guys from Jennifer. The gal that owns Arnold's."

"Small town, I reckon" Chris said in his best southern drawl. The grown ups laughed but the kids didn't understand why.

Following lunch, Chris and the kids parked their car at grandma Pat's and strolled into town to search the book shelves of Downtown Books. It was Linda's practice that during the summer months the kids would read at least three books and Chris decided to keep that tradition alive, even if Linda wasn't. Jamie picked out a mystery book by local author Joseph LS Terrell, Eric got a book about Blackbeard the Pirate, who once long ago roamed the waters of the North Carolina coast and Savannah went with a book about puppies and kitties. Chris selected a trivia book, Figured he could use it somehow on the air. It was "The Andy Griffith Show" Complete Trivia Guide, by local author, Greg Smrdel.

With books in hand the family walked the block back to grandma Pat's, stopping along the way at the house they'll be moving into tomorrow. Chris had the keys in his pocket so they all went inside. It was stuffy, so Chris turned the air conditioner onto a setting of 72 degrees to cool it down a bit. The kids all ran upstairs and started picking out their rooms.

"Daddy, this is my room!" Savannah shouted.

"Well, pumpkin, We have three bedrooms in this house so you and Jamie are going to have to share a room." Chris continued, "Jamie, I'm sorry we didn't discuss ahead time. You ok with that? I promise it will only be for this year, when we buy a house it will be with 4 bedrooms."

"Sure no problem." Jamie said "come on squirt, let's find our room."

"Jamie, I was thinking that since you and Savannah have to share that you two should have the master bedroom. It's the biggest of the rooms and you guys will each have your own closet and a bathroom. It can be the girls bathroom."

"Eric, you and I will take these two rooms, with the Jack-and-Jill bathroom."

Tickled by that, Savannah let out a squeal. "Haha, we have a girls bathroom and so does Eric!"

"What are you talking about dork?"

"Daddy has a Jack bathroom and you have a Jill bathroom. "Cause you're a *giiiiirl.* "

"And you're a dork."

"Ok kids, enough, let's go back to grandma Pat's now. We'll be moving in here tomorrow, and for now, let's hang around the pool."

"That's a good idea daddy."

"Thanks pumpkin."

The family spent the rest of the afternoon hanging out at grandma Pat's pool either reading or splashing around. Eric was even a decent big brother for part of the day helping to teach Savannah how to swim. Being on swim team, Eric is always talking about being a lifeguard and a swim coach at some point in his life.

At 5:00, Chris announced that it was time to go inside, start taking showers and getting dressed for the party that night. Jamie and Savannah took turns in the upstairs shower; Chris and Eric taking turns in the outdoor shower. Following his shower, it was Eric that asked what would happen if they were outside taking a shower and a snake slithered into the shower stall. Chris said he didn't know, but thanks for putting that thought into my head....

The kids were showered and dressed into some clean clothes, when somewhere just past 6:00, Storm called Jamie's cell phone and asked if she could come down and walk with the family to Arnold's.

"Sure you can!" Said Jamie, feeling a bit better about the move having another older girl that she could look up to.

"Great" Storm answered. "I'll see you in five minutes."

Soon Chris, grandma Pat, Jamie, Eric, Savannah and Storm were ready to leave for the "welcome home party." Jennifer had worked all day and was already there getting everything together. The kids wanted to walk together the half-mile to the restaurant, while Chris and grandma Pat decided to drive since it would be later when they would be coming home, and safer to drive rather than walk back in the dark.

Grandma Pat and Chris got there at the same time as Annie and Greg Gray, and John Clark. Already inside were JW and Bonnie Bennett. Chris decided he would wait in a rocking chair outside until the kids arrived. It was the same chair he sat in a few months ago while agonizing over the decision to move or not to move. Chris didn't need to wait more the five minutes when he saw the kids come up the street and into the parking lot, led by Savannah who was having a great time, pretending she was in charge.

"I got us all here daddy" said Savannah. "I remembered all by myself how to get here."

"That's great pumpkin. I am so proud of you."

"Thanks daddy." But Savannah couldn't leave it there. She had to follow it up with "see Eric? Daddy is always proud of me. He never says that about you…"

"Dork."

"See Storm, this is what my life is…." Savannah said to the older neighbor. The sheer silliness of that statement coming from an elementary school aged child made the others double over laughing.

Savannah, not knowing what the fuss was about, merely said, "let's go in. I'm hungry."

The party that night was fabulous. The food was outstanding. Jennifer even remembered to include Chris' favorite, East Carolina Barbecue. There was also spiced shrimp, seared scallops, fried oysters and blackened grouper for the adults and chicken nuggets, mac and cheese and hamburgers for the kids. Everyone ate like it would be their last meal.

Somewhere around 9:30 the party started breaking up. The next day was still a work day for John, the Gray's and the Bennett's. As everyone began to go their separate ways, John told everyone to be sure and stop by Dare Day on Saturday around noon for a major announcement. Of course, this being the circle of friends, they already knew what that announcement was going to be, but promised to come out for support nonetheless.

Grandma Pat loaded up the kids and Storm into her car for the drive home. Chris decided to stay behind. He was going to help Jennifer clean up from the party and would catch a ride back with her.

Grandma Pat with a twinkle in her eye said, "just remember, big day tomorrow for you too son. The movers will be there in the morning."

"I know ma. Just not fair to leave all this work on Jennifer. I won't be late."

CHAPTER 30.

Chris had a fitful night of sleep. He often did when something big was looming the next day. He had always been like that, never being able to turn off his brain sometimes. He had been awaken by an early morning text from the movers. They have left Herndon, Virginia and were on their way. Arrival time of about 10:30. They wanted to be on and off the Outer Banks before the weekend traffic would arrive.

Chris stood up and stretched. He threw on some shorts and a t-shirt and made his way downstairs. He knew his mother would already have the coffee going and having her first cup.

"Morning Chris" grandma Pat said as Chris reached the main floor. "Big day today."

"Yeah, the movers are already on their way, should be here around 10:30 or so. I'm going to grab a shower and a cup of coffee and head over to the house and get ready for them."

"What about the kids? You want me to keep them here and out of the way? Or do you want me to bring them over and help with the moving?"

"Probably best to keep them out of the way. The movers made it sound like they want to unload quickly and be off the Outer Banks before it gets too crazy later this afternoon."

"Ok. When they wake up, I'll take them down to Poor Richards for a quick breakfast. We'll swing by your house afterwards with a sweet potato biscuit and a coffee for you."

"Thanks ma." With that, Chris downed the last of the coffee in his cup and started downstairs to shower outside. "When I come back up, I'm going to have a another cup, so please don't turn off the pot yet."

"No worries son."

Chris took his time outside showering. He still had a couple of hours before the crew would be along to the house, and there wasn't much he could do before then. After about 20 minutes Chris toweled off, slipped back into his shorts and t-shirt and went back upstairs for his second coffee of the day.

"No kids awake yet?" Chris asked his mother.

"Not yet. Haven't heard a peep. Been a long and hectic couple of days for them. Let them sleep as late as they want. Nothing they need to get up for anyway."

"Yeah, true. After I finish this coffee I'm going to head over to the house. You have a couple of rags and cleaning supplies I can use? I want to wipe down counters and do the windows before the furniture starts arriving."

"Look under the sink. You should find everything you need. Good idea about the windows, maybe you could do mine this week for me. The salty air has a tendency to leave a film on them after a while."

With a slight roll to his eyes, which grandma Pat caught, Chris replied, "yeah, I'll take care of that in my spare time."

After finishing his coffee, Chris grabbed the rags, Windex, Lysol All-Purpose cleaner, and his bluetooth speaker and walked over to his new house on Croatan Avenue to clean and wait on the movers.

Using his cell phone, Chris hooked to the speaker and put on Ocean 105. John Clark happened to be on the air and was talking about Uncle Danny being out at Dare Day tomorrow and that Ocean 105 had a major programming announcement. For the first time since the whole moving back and taking Uncle Danny's air shift had come up, Chris felt a tinge of nerves. Questions like "how do I fill Uncle Danny's shoes?" and "what if everyone hates me?" Started to cloud Chris' mind. "What if this doesn't work out? Then what?" He further wondered.

His concentration broken by a loud knock on the front door. Being upstairs, Chris didn't see who it was exactly, but he heard who ever it was let themselves in.

"Hello? Anybody home?" The voice called out.

Chris recognized the voice. It was Jennifer stopping by to check on things no doubt. "Hey upstairs," Chris called down to her.

Jennifer bounded up the stairs. She had on a pair of cut-off jean shorts, a tie-dyed tank top and a bandanna tied around her head. Chris met her at the top of the stair case and let out a mock "eww."

"Yeah, jerk. I come over to help and you go eww? What kind of friend are you going to turn out to be?"

"What do you mean help?"

"Yeah. I took the day off from the restaurant. Got my manager running it today. I figured you would have your hands full so I came to help. Storm is over at your mom's. She's gonna help with the kids there."

Chris taken aback by this said, "I don't even want to be here doing this. Why would you want to?"

"Now, don't get me wrong. I don't *want* to be here doing this either. I'd much rather be over at Fish Heads having a margarita on my day off. But I figure if I spend a few hours over here helping then you'll have to buy me one of those margaritas the next time I go."

"Hmmm, devious woman. I'm going to have to keep my eye on you."

They both laughed, then Jennifer grabbed some rags and the Lysol and started cleaning the bathroom. "I haven't seen a man yet that can clean a bathroom right."

Chris went around cleaning the windows. At first, he didn't really think they needed it, but when done he was really able to tell the difference. "There," he said about an hour and a half later, done and ready to go. He looked at his watch. It was about 10:15. The movers would be along shortly so he and Jennifer had a seat on the front steps. Just then Chris and Jennifer noticed Storm, Jamie and Savannah, hand-in-hand coming down the adjacent street, followed by Eric and grandma Pat bringing up the rear.

"Hey daddy, we're going to Poor Ricky's for breakfast" Savannah yelled out.

"It's Poor Richard's dork." Eric said correcting his sister.

"Oh yeah, it's Poor Richard's. Grandma said we can bring you a biscuit and coffee on our way back. Can we get you something too Miss Jennifer?"

"Sure Savannah. Thanks. Can I also get a biscuit and coffee?"

"Yes, Miss Jennifer. I'll tell my grandma Pat. You don't have to have money either, cause she has lots of it. I saw she had three, twenty dollar bills this morning!"

Laughing, Jennifer thanked Savannah as the kids made their way down the block to Poor Richards. From their vantage point on the front steps they could see the party of five as they disappeared into the restaurant.

"Sweet kid" Jennifer said about Savannah.

"Yeah, she is" Chris replied. "Just no filter on her sometimes."

"Well Chris, little girls will be little girls."

"Reckon they will be" Chris said.

Just then, the moving truck that Chris last saw three days ago at his old house on Hibiscus Court in Westerville, Ohio came clanking through downtown slowly as though they were looking for an address. Chris got up from the front porch steps, went out into the middle of the street and guided them in.

The yellow house on Croatan Avenue was a corner house. The driveway located on the adjacent Devon Street, making it a further walk from truck to house. Thankfully Chris had labeled each box as to where it belonged when he packed, making it that much easier to put it in the right spot in the new house. Jennifer stayed in the house directing traffic as to what went into what room. Chris, in order to make the day go quicker, helped the two movers unload the truck. They apparently were unaccustomed to getting such help from the client, by gladly accepted it, making their day that much easier.

As the last box made it into the house, Chris looked at the time on his cellphone. Almost 2:30 pm. The movers were pleased. They figured they could be back at their home base in Richmond, Virginia in time for dinner. Chris was also pleased, but knew he still had a mountain of work ahead of him. Because the movers agreed to assemble all the beds for Chris when they unloaded them, he handed them a $100 tip before they left.

Once the movers climbed back up into their truck, hit the engine and started on their journey home, Chris turned his attention to unpacking. Jennifer volunteered to set up the kitchen while Chris went upstairs and started making all the beds and putting the family's clothes away. He put towels in the linen closet and hung a shower curtain in each of the bathrooms.

Jennifer and Chris worked through the afternoon until about 6 or so. At that point Eric and Savannah walked over to the new house to check everything out. Savannah still making sure that she and Jamie got "the big room." They did. She also made sure to take the opportunity to let Miss Jennifer know that Eric's bathroom was a girl's bathroom because it was named "Jill."

"Dork."

"Daddy, grandma Pat said for you and Miss Jennifer to come over and that you have to start the grill." Savannah said proudly as she carried out her instructions well.

"What am I supposed to do Savannah?" Jennifer asked.

"Grandma said you're not supposed to do anything. She said you probably did all the work today and that you're supposed to sit down and let daddy make you dinner."

Chris groaned and Jennifer laughed as they closed the door on the yellow house and walked back to grandma Pat's.

When Chris and the group got to grandma Pat's, they found Storm and Jamie making the salad for the dinner. Grandma Pat would have made an excellent drill sergeant, Chris often thought. As soon as Eric and Savannah made their way back up the elevator and into the kitchen, grandma Pat handed them seven ears of corn and told them to go outside to husk them. She didn't want the mess in her house. Next, she handed Chris a bottle of wine and a platter containing three tuna steaks, which she had picked up earlier in the day at the seafood market in Wanchese. It also had a pack of hot dogs to put on the grill for the kids. Her instructions were to first open the bottle of wine and pour two glasses. One for her and one for Jennifer so they could sit down and relax, then to go down to the pool and put the tuna steaks on the grill. Before heading out, Chris grabbed a Red Stripe for himself out of the refrigerator and took it with hm as he rode the elevator to the ground floor.

His mom had already started the grill before Chris had gotten there, so it was just a matter of throwing the food on it and letting it cook. A well prepared tuna steak should be served medium-rare, so it shouldn't take much time at all.

With a belly full of tuna, corn and salad, Chris was feeling content as he rounded up the kids, said their goodbyes and walked back to their yellow house around the corner on Croatan Avenue. It will be their first night in their new home in their new place. Chris got each kid into their pajamas, got them to brush their teeth. While helping Savannah get ready for bed, he was taken aback. He didn't know if it was the light, or what it was, but in looking at his youngest daughter, he saw his late wife when Savannah said, "daddy, we're home aren't we?"

Wiping a tear from his eye, the young child's father replied, "yes pumpkin we are."

That night, Chris had the best night of sleep that he's had in quite some time.

CHAPTER 31.

Chris was startled awake by the noise of activity coming from downtown, a mere two houses away from his. There was the sound of garbage trucks making a last sweep of the dumpsters, making sure everything was empty in anticipation of today's crowd. There was some last minute hammering to get the stages set throughout the town, and the voices of men and women as they shouted to each other across the streets from underneath their canopies they've erected so they may set up their vendor tables. It is Dare Day in Manteo! It all gets underway in two hours at 9:00 am.

Savannah walked sleepily into Chris' room. "Daddy? Are we going to the fair today?"

"Yes we are princess. Remember, I have to work for the radio station today for a little bit, but while I'm working, you and Jamie and Eric can go on some rides and walk around. I want you guys there at the radio station booth when we make our big announcement today."

"You mean the announcement of Radio Disney daddy? Remember, I said you can tell them it was your idea!"

"No pumpkin. They're going to announce that I'm the new DJ."

"Oh, so they'll talk about Radio Disney later then…."

Thankfully, Eric woke up and came into the bedroom through the jack and jill bathroom. "Hahaha, look daddy! Eric was just in his *girlie* bathroom!"

"Be quiet dork."

"Ok guys. Why don't you two be quiet so you don't wake up your sister. Go downstairs and let me take a shower. Then I'll get breakfast going.

"Ok pops, but just one thing," Eric said, "You haven't gone grocery shopping yet, so there is nothing for breakfast."

"Good point boy. As soon as I'm showered and dressed, we'll make a run to McDonalds."

Chris got up, went outside, got in his shower. He toweled off and dressed. He loaded his two youngest in the Jeep, deciding to let Jamie stay home and sleep, and made their way to Mickey D's. Since the McDonald's was out on Highway 64, outside of the downtown area, it should be relatively easy to get to. Chris rolled the Jeep through the drive-thru and ordered four, number ones. Egg McMuffin's with hash browns. One with a large coffee, one with orange juice for Jamie, and two with chocolate milk for Eric and Savannah.

The trio got back home, Savannah went upstairs to get Jamie up and the family had their first meal around their old kitchen table in their new house. Too bad it had to be fast food.

Dare Day is a big deal in Manteo. It's a day, mostly for the locals, that takes place on the first Saturday of every June on the waterfront in Manteo. There is a big stage out in front of what used to be the courthouse, but is now the headquarters for the Dare County Arts Council. But everyone still calls it the old courthouse. From that stage, there will be a blessing of the season at 9:00 am that will kick off the day of celebration.

Before the day is over at 6:00 pm, that stage will have seen ten different acts performing. The Boathouse Stage will also see a host of acts throughout the day. Also at Dare Days this year there will be racing pigs, blue ribbon contests, "anything that floats boat races," a kids zone, and a bike stunt show.

Off the beaten path, will be Uncle Danny, broadcasting live from the amphitheater in Festival Park, on Ice Plant Island. This will provide a bit of a quieter location while at the same time, provide a large grass area where visitors to Dare Day may come, stretch out a blanket and enjoy a leisurely picnic lunch while listening to the Uncle and Ocean 105.

The radio station for a week now had been running a "big announcement" promo seemingly every ten minutes. They're expecting a large crowd to gather, hence needing the space at the amphitheater.

It was 8:30 when the family finished their non-nutritious breakfast and cleaned away the food wrappers. Still thirty minutes before the opening of Dare Day. Chris decided to take the kids into town and show them where the amphitheater was so they knew where to be at noon. The family walked across the bridge to Ice Plant Island. At the crest of the bridge, there were a group of 5 boys, each around Eric's age, jumping from the structure into Shallowbag Bay below. Chris saw the twinkle in Eric's eye as he muttered "sweet" to himself. Chris had no doubt that his son would fit right in here.

Chris led the family past the parking lot and museum store and through the gates to the amphitheater. A beautiful location for his first day on the air. From the grassy area, you can see through the stage to the sparkling waters of the Roanoke Sound behind it. A gentle breeze was blowing through, taking the humidity of the day with it. Chris noticed that the radio station van was parked to the left of the stage and the engineer was busily getting everything plugged in and ready for the broadcast.

The station promotion department was out hanging the big "BIG ANNOUNCEMENT TODAY AT NOON" banner over the arch at the top of the stage. Won't be any subtlety in this, Chris thought to himself.

"Ok guys" Chris said to his three kids. "If we go in separate directions this morning, this is where I want you to be at noon, ok?"

"Daddy, I may be having too much fun to remember, you better have Jamie be in charge" Savannah said.

"No worries squirt. I set my alarm on my phone for 11:45 so we can make it here in time."

Chris, looking at his son, knowing his plan was to hook up with the neighborhood boys to do some bridge jumping said, "you too boy. I mean it. Don't make me ground you on our first week here."

"Don't worry papadopoulos. I'll be here."

"Good. I hope so."

Chris and the kids turned and made their way out of Festival Park and back over to the waterfront. The celebration was ready to kick-off in ten minutes. As they crossed back over the bridge they ran into grandma Pat, Jennifer and Storm as they walked into town.

"Nervous about the big announcement today, Chris?" Jennifer asked.

"I wouldn't say nervous, but I just wished they would have down played this thing a little. I'm already starting in a hole trying to fill Uncle Danny's shoes. Now I have to overcome all this hype too."

"Oh, son, you'll be fine. Now who wants to go with grandma Pat to find some cotton candy?"

In unison, all four kids; Jamie, Eric, Savannah and Storm shouted "I do!"

"At this time of day mom? My how you have changed since I was a kid."

"Oh hush up son. I'm allowed to spoil these younguns. Why don't you and Jennifer go over to Poor Richards and grab a cup of coffee."

"Ok mom, but please make sure they are all at the amphitheater by noon."

"Don't worry son. We'll all be there."

Grandma Pat and the kids turned down Budleigh Street in search of the spun sugar treats and Chris and Jennifer entered Poor Richards from the boardwalk of the water through the back door.

Although having already eaten his McDonald's breakfast, he still ordered a sweet potato biscuit and a large coffee. Jennifer, who apparently hadn't eaten yet, ordered the breakfast burrito, hash browns and a large coffee. Luckily they were able to get a spot at a table on the small rear deck of the restaurant overlooking the marina.

Chris started the conversation, "I would have figured you would be working today."

"Nah," Jennifer answered. "Everyone in town spends their day down here. Generally a slow day for the restaurant so I close every year during Dare Day. That way the staff can enjoy it too."

"Oh nice." Chris replied. "I love this Dare Day celebration. I missed it when we moved back to Ohio. Nothing like that there unfortunately."

"Yeah, I'll bet" Jennifer responded. "Big day for you though, huh?"

"Yeah. I guess. I'm looking forward to hitting the air on Monday and get this thing going finally."

"Wow, look at me. Having breakfast with a bonafide *celebrity*!" The way Jennifer put the emphasis on the "Cee" part of the word, informed Chris that she was joking.

"Yeah, I'm a big deal." He said. "I'm only another schlep just trying to do his best to make it through this life."

Jennifer and Chris finished up their breakfast and strolled back to the festivities. They missed the blessing of the season but got to the courthouse stage in time to see the first band start their set. Three songs in, Chris and Jennifer decided to stroll the streets of downtown. Look at the vendor offerings since Chris still needed to decorate the yellow house down the street. Jennifer volunteered to help pick out some things for him. Glad for the help, they picked out some wall furnishings and a couple of knickknacks. Wanting to change his clothes before joining Uncle Danny at the broadcast booth, the two walked back to the yellow house, put the day's booty on the kitchen table and Chris went up stairs to change into khaki pants, a golf shirt and boat shoes.

It was approaching 11:30 now so Chris figured he better make his way over to the amphitheater. Now the nerves started to kick in as the butterflies started flying around his stomach. Those thoughts about whether he made the right decision for his family or not started swirling around his brain.. The fear of the unknown is a powerful thing and Chris was succumbing to it fast.

Jennifer and Chris walked towards downtown, turned left onto the bridge leading to Festival Park. At the foot of the bridge, along the waterfront in front of The 1587 Inn, Chris noticed the Bennett's walking his way. Chris and Jennifer waited for them to catch up and the four walked over the bridge together. Outside the gate to the amphitheater, milling about with the crowd, it was Jennifer who spotted the Gray's. She called out to them, and the six walked in together.

"Nervous?" JW Bennett wanted to know.

"Not sure nervous is the right word, but a bit uneasy." Chris answered.

As he made his way to the broadcast area on the stage of the amphitheater, Chris heard someone call out his name. He didn't recognize the person right away, but it turned out to be someone that recognized him from his previous stint at the radio station.

"You part of the big announcement?" The fan wanted to know.

Smiling sheepishly, Chris just responded "we'll see," and thanked the listener for being there and went onto the stage.

"Bro!" John greeted Chris. "Perfect timing! We're just about to hit the airwaves."

"Hey Chris, good to see you. You ready for this?" Asked Uncle Danny.

"I just hope I can fill your shoes Danny. They are some huge shoes to fill. I hope I'm not setting both the station and my family up for failure here."

"Chris, you have nothing to worry about. You were great when you did mornings here. You continue to be community-oriented and they will love you again."

"I hope so Danny, but you're like a legend here. I can't imagine Ocean 105 without you."

"Me neither Bros," John chimed in, "but its time for a new era, and all of us are pulling for you and support you 100%."

"Thanks John, that's nice to hear."

The clock indicated it was 11:59:30 AM. The onsite producer counted down the time to noon. Chris looked out at the crowd. He saw his mother. He saw his kids. He saw his friends, both old and new. There were about 1,500 crammed into the grassy area. Some on chairs, some on blankets enjoying their lunch, most standing in front of the stage. Shouts of "Hey Uncle Danny!" With Danny waving out at the crowd. Danny looked over to Chris sitting on his right side, winked and said, "soon they'll be doing this for you son."

Just then, the clock struck noon. The producer signaled for the start of the live broadcast. The speakers erupted with the sound of Roman trumpets, the type that used to play Don Rickles onstage in Vegas at the start of his show. Approximately twenty seconds into the music, Uncle Danny launched into:

"Good afternoon! Broadcasting live from the amphitheater at Festival Park in Manteo its your Uncle Danny on Ocean 105!"

Cheers from those standing in front of the stage were picked up on the microphone and broadcast out onto the station.

Uncle Danny continued, "We promised you a major announcement and we won't keep you waiting. Today will be your Uncle's last broadcast. I am retiring from Ocean 105 after nearly 40 years on the air!"

Choruses of boos started erupting from the crowd started filtering up to the stage. Uncle Danny now standing holding his hands up, so he can continue to speak, a loud, "We love you Uncle Danny!" Was yelled out from the crowd.

"Aww, shucks, your Uncle Danny loves you too, but I want to let ya'll know, I ain't goin' nowhere. I will still be here on the Outer Banks, just not on the radio no more. Today I want to introduce my replacement. Some of you folks may remember him from a few years ago when he did the morning show here. He'll be the new afternoon DJ beginning day after tomorrow. Ladies and gentleman, I want you to know my good friend, and soon to be yours, Chris Stephens!........"

…..To be continued.

About The Author

Greg Smrdel is a comedian, writer and contributor for "My Outer Banks Home." His comedy can be seen nationwide at comedy clubs, casinos and in theaters.

www.gregsmrdel.com

Made in the USA
Lexington, KY
03 September 2018